URCELIA TEIXEIRA

A JORJA ROSE CHRISTIAN THRILLER

VALLEY OF DEATH SERIES BOOK 1 OF 3

VENGEANCE IS MINE

VENGEANCE IS MINE
A JORJA ROSE CHRISTIAN SUSPENSE THRILLER

VALLEY OF DEATH BOOK I

by URCELIA TEIXEIRA

Copyrighted material
E-book © ISBN: 978-1-928537-76-2
Paperback © ISBN: 978-1-928537-77-9
Independently Published by Urcelia Teixeira

First edition

Urcelia Teixeira, Wiltshire, UK

www.urcelia.com

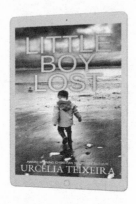

*To the valued members of the
'Between my Pages' Facebook group,
Your ongoing prayers and encouragement
motivate and keep my eyes focused on the amazing
God we serve!
Thank you for your ceaseless support.
You are near and dear to my heart!*

INSPIRED BY

"It is mine to avenge; I will repay. In due time their foot will slip; their day of disaster is near and their doom rushes upon them."
Deuteronomy 32:35
(NIV)

PREFACE

Before you read...

This book is the first part of a three-part story that spans across all three books in the Valley of Death series. It is a true trilogy, meaning there will be a cliffhanger ending at the end of this book, Vengeance is Mine, and again at the end of the second book, Shadow of Fear before you find the resolution you seek at the end of the final book, Wages of Sin.

What you will not find at the end of this first install-ment is a perfect conclusion, but you will find a pulse-pounding read you won't want to put down once you start. One that will provide solid threads of faith, twists, turns, and toe-curling thrills to set the stage for what's coming!

If you stick with me and read all three books in this tril-ogy, I promise you will get that heart-in-my-throat-never-saw-that-coming ending that will wrap up in an explosive finale guaranteed to satisfy and release the tense build-up you will experience throughout Jorja Rose's journey.

Buckle up, dear reader, sit back in your favorite chair, and be prepared for an epic binge-read!

CHAPTER ONE

They say the truth shall set you free, but that's a lie. Her truth had not set her free at all. Jorja Rose was in captivity. Held prisoner by her conscience. Perhaps even guilt.

Her mind was in an unyielding state of war as she fought a never-ending battle between good and evil. A battle she did not know how to win, or even if she could ever win. She was trapped. Caught between the person she once was and the one she had worked so hard to create. For nearly twenty years she had battled a secret war she had buried deep within, hidden from all who now knew her, pushed into the darkest corners of her soul, where no one could ever see it.

There were days—one too many if she was honest with herself—where she found herself missing her past life.

Almost yearning for it, at times. The adrenaline that surged through her veins, the rush of tempting fate, and the victory that came at the end. Memories of what she once had, were sweet, as were the bitterness and despair of what could have been.

Now, her life tended toward boredom at the best of times. Sometimes she hardly recognized the person she'd been forced to become. But it was what needed to be done, to keep her alive.

Ironically, her deception was also what snuffed the inner torture and led her to discover that there was a higher power, a God who knew it all and cling to the hope it could bring—one day. But surrendering all meant that her secrets would be unveiled, her truth exposed and the precise retribution she had been running from all these years, unleashed.

And so it continued. The perpetual loop of her past was holding her back from experiencing a future in true freedom. Blocked and trapped in a grip that would never let her go.

But then she also knew she was not ready to let go. There was too much she still longed for. Too much she still missed. But, this life had chosen her. It was the bed she had made and she had found respite in that, built her hedge around her, locked the past away, and stepped into a world of pretense.

To all who had come to know her in the tranquil

English fishing village she'd called home for more than two decades now, she was as close to God as anyone on earth could strive to be. But in the deep corners of her soul Jorja knew the truth, the whole truth. She was a fraud. Someone who lived a twisted lie and deceived those who had taught her what it meant to truly love—and be loved. Like a festering sore it had eaten away at her soul, slowly devouring her, leaving her living in fear instead of freedom. The kind of fear that leaves you looking over your shoulder, always expecting the worst, waiting for your day of reckoning. By man... or by God.

Even there, in the hidden corners at the very edge of Cornwall, England, she had never felt safe. Nor did she know if she ever would again.

FROM BEHIND THE white marble counter in her small art gallery, she stared through the large window at the man who stood across the street. He'd been standing there for hours, watching her shop. At first, she'd thought he was admiring the painting in her window—a large oil-painted scene of a young woman staring out across the rugged Cornish coastline. It was easy to get lost in its beauty and not unusual for visitors to stop and admire. But something about this man seemed odd. She had lived on the peninsula long enough to know he wasn't one of them. Nor was he one of the regulars who visited their village on week-ends or during the summer. He was tall, at the very least six foot, but if she had to guess, closer to six three. Someone like that stood out from the crowd. And it left her unsettled. There was something dark about his stance, threatening, foreboding.

His camel-colored coat draped snugly over his broad shoulders and beneath it, he wore a black button-up shirt and matching black slacks. From where she stood, she could not quite make out his face but his bald head was unmissable.

She fumbled with the sticky tape between her fingers as she wrapped the last piece of tissue paper around the eight by twelve-inch watercolor canvas in front of her. *Why did this man make her so nervous?* Deep in thought, she botched a strip of tape, tearing the corner of the wrapping paper as she shot another cautious glance at the man across the street.

"Is everything all right, Jorja?" Myles Brentwood inquired. "You look a little on edge this afternoon." He would know. He was a regular at her shop and the art teacher at their local secondary school. Of average build and in his mid-sixties, Myles grew up in St. Ives and happily worked the same teaching job he had started back in his late twenties.

"Yes, yes, I'm fine, sorry. Must be the cold that's getting to my fingers," she replied, flashing him a sideways smile as she grabbed a new sheet of paper.

"Indeed, fall has come very early this year it seems. I

had hoped to squeeze in a couple more trips to capture the new school of seals on Godrevy Island, but as we all know by now, these winds could turn on a dime and leave me stranded out there with Henry for who knows how long. God bless the boy but he is too much of a talker when he takes that rusty trawler of his out to sea. My desire to capture the island's magic on canvas is great, but not that critical. Art is best enjoyed in silence, you know." He chuckled. "Which reminds me, I was hoping you could stop by my class next week to give the kids your thoughts on our friend, Da Vinci? This year's kids are brimming with potential, an intellectual bunch if I dare to venture so early in the academic year."

Jorja didn't answer as she slipped his neatly wrapped monthly purchase into the gift bag and handed it to him.

"So, would you?" Myles pushed again when she didn't answer.

"Would I what?"

"Impart your wisdom to the class. Did you not hear a word I said, Jorja? You seem a little distracted. Are you sure you're not coming down with something?"

"Of course, sorry, yes," she spluttered, knowing full well his suspicions were spot on. She was distracted, by the man across the street.

She tore her attention back to her customer.

"I'll be happy to pop by anytime, Myles. Now that most of our visitors have left I can slip away from the shop for an hour or so."

"Excellent, that'll do just fine, thank you. If they don't bombard you with questions you should have it wrapped up in under forty minutes."

He turned toward the exit, parcel in hand, then suddenly turned back to look at her.

"You know, Jorja, I don't think I've ever told you. I think everyone was very wrong about you back then. This town of ours is blessed to have you. I don't know why we all gave you such a hard time when you first got here. Before you came along this town was dead, but this little gallery of yours gave us all life, put us on the map, so to speak. You have been nothing but a strength to our community. Small-town mentality is what it was. Or, if I'm brutally honest, it might have been your leather attire that had you looking like you were up to no good." He chuckled then continued. "But you've certainly proven these gossiping geese wrong, haven't you?" He winked as if he had just told her a secret.

"Well, I'll be off then." He turned back to the door as he muttered, "Got a dreaded faculty meeting in fifteen minutes. Always so much talking at these things."

The wood-framed glass door shut behind him and she watched as he crossed the street to where he briefly paused in front of the strange man opposite the shop. Almost intentionally, Myles looked him square in the face then said something she couldn't make out. Knowing him it was most likely a hearty welcome since he served on the town committee and was notorious for making their visitors feel welcome.

The stranger didn't reciprocate and instead, promptly walked off in the opposite direction. As he did so, Myles looked back at Jorja and tipped his head forward in the slightest of nods as if to say she shouldn't worry, he had taken care of her. A quick wave of her hand thanked him before she watched him settle into a steady stroll back in the direction of the school.

Yes, Myles Brentwood was an old soul, but a wise one nonetheless, and his alert observation was so typical of how the residents of St. Ives always looked out for one another.

But, while knowing that her safety in the village should have provided her with peace, it didn't.

She glanced at her watch. There was another hour or so to go before closing time, and she had intended on stopping by the supermarket to pick up a few groceries before heading home. If she waited until then, she would be walking home as dusk set in. Ordinarily, that would not have deterred her, but today, she wasn't sure she was prepared to risk it. Deciding she would close the shop early, she rushed over to the door, glanced up and down the street to make sure the man was gone, then dashed back behind the marble shop counter to find her purse. Her heart had snuck into her throat where it quickened to a pulsating sense of dread.

"Stop it!" she admonished herself out loud, setting her

purse atop the counter as she shut her eyes and took a deep breath in an attempt to pull herself together.

She told herself it wasn't possible. It had been too long. She was halfway across the world and not even her parents knew she was still alive; a deliberate choice she'd been compelled to make. For her own protection, and theirs.

CHAPTER TWO

S he set off on her morning run earlier than usual. Her sleep had been interrupted by her tabby, Vincent—unashamedly named after Van Gogh because he was missing the tip of one of his ears. Vincent had darted off her bed at the crack of dawn, chased down the passage, and gone into hiding under the guest bedroom bed as if something had frightened him. When Jorja eventually unlocked his cat door and stepped out onto her porch he dashed past her legs and disappeared into the bordering bushes.

Her feet hit the road in a comfortable rhythm as she took her usual route down toward the bay that soon appeared in full view in front of her. Above her, the sky was hinting at a sunny day, and early morning seagulls squawked noisily above a dark shoal of fish just below the ocean's surface. At forty-eight, Jorja was still in top shape and looked ten years younger. After she came to live in St. Ives she had kept up her training routine; ten-mile runs every day at 7 a.m. and an hour of Pilates on her living room floor in the evening, never missing a single day. Superficially, she had always told herself it was because she liked how it felt to be healthy, but if she was truthful, she knew the real reason was that she wanted to be ready, clinging to the hope that she would one day return.

AN ONLY CHILD of two blue-collar workers she'd run away from their modest English home at sixteen, dropping out of school after she traveled to Paris for the first time on a school trip to visit The Louvre. It was where she had first fallen in love with art, and all it came to offer in the years that followed.

When she returned home after the trip she would sneak away from school as often as she could, taking the train to London to roam the corridors of the National Gallery. There, in Room 43, she would lose herself in Van Gogh's paintings, and eventually, it was where she would also lose her heart. Her life was never the same again after she met him.

She had stolen money from her parents' rainy-day fund to pay for her train ticket to Paris and a few months' rent; silently vowing she would pay back every penny. And she did, with interest, in the form of an anonymous monthly check that enabled her parents to pay off their mortgage and retire early with change to spare. As far as she knew, they still lived in the same terrace house in Newcastle. Forced to break all ties when she moved to St. Ives she had not spoken to them since. For all she knew they had already passed.

AS SHE TURNED the corner toward the coastal path that weaved its way along the sea cliffs, her name wafted in the breeze toward her and brought her to a sudden halt. She removed her AirPods and turned to see her friend fighting for her attention at the top of the road. Ewan beckoned her to come over and seemed excessively eager to speak to her so she ran toward him. He had been her best friend for the better part of fifteen years and despite the townsfolk's speculation that they were romantically involved, they had remained just close friends. He was also the town's commanding law enforcement officer, formally ranked as detective inspector.

"You're out early," he said as they neared each other, by now familiar with Jorja's running schedule.

"Couldn't sleep so I thought I'd get an early start. What's up that couldn't wait until I got back home?"

His face went grim beneath his handsome features.

"There was an incident."

"What type of incident?" She cocked her head to one side, wiping away a few beads of sweat that trickled down her left temple.

"A murder."

"A murder? You're joking. Here, in St. Ives?"

"Afraid not. Times are changing, I guess." His eyes narrowed as he held her eyes with his.

"Why are you looking at me like that? Who was it?"

"Myles Brentwood."

His green eyes remained fixed on hers as if he was prompting her for answers.

"What? When? How?" she rattled off, stunned by the information.

"We're guessing sometime last night, but we're not sure of anything just yet. My men are processing the crime scene as we speak and I'm still waiting for the forensic team to arrive."

Jorja rested both hands on her hips as she stared out across the ocean.

"Wow, I just saw him yesterday."

"I know." Ewan stared uncomfortably at his feet then looked up, struggling to find the words.

"Why are you looking at me like that, Ewan Reid? What's going on?"

He attempted to speak then stopped himself, drawing a deep breath instead.

"Spit it out, Ewan," she pushed, sensing he was holding out on her.

"I'm sorry, Jorgie, but I have to ask. It's my job."

He took one deep breath for courage and forced the words from his mouth.

"Where were you yesterday between five p.m. and sunrise?"

His face flushed as soon as the words left his lips.

Jorja's body tensed and she briefly turned her back on him before she spun around to face him.

"How long have we known each other, Ewan, huh? Do you honestly think I am capable of killing someone?"

He didn't answer, pushing the fragile boundaries of their friendship once more. He was torn between loyalty to his job and his best friend and, in all his years on the force, had never once thought he would have to challenge it in this way. But so far, what little evidence they had gathered during the night all pointed to her.

"I was home, alone, like I am every night. You of all people should know that by now."

She crossed her arms, her eyes filled with hurt.

Ewan's voice became gentle. "You were the last person to see him alive, Jorgie. I'm sorry, it's my job. I have to make sure I have all the facts before Major Crimes gets here. It's not like we have a murder here every week, you know. I'm sorry, okay?"

She stepped away from him again, her back toward him once more.

"Why don't you just tell me what you know, Jorgie, then I can move on and catch the guy who did this? Why did you close your shop early?"

Jorja threw her head back in disbelief as she turned and flashed an amused smile, knowing it could have only been Jenny from the flower shop next door that could have told him.

"That's the thing with our little town. Everyone knows everyone's business. Did Jenny also tell you that Myles was very much alive when he left my shop? And that I popped by Ann's to pick up some fresh milk and a tin of cat food for Vincent."

Ewan nodded.

"Well, then I don't understand, Ewan. I'm trying to stay calm here but I guess I am just a little offended that you of all people could think I am capable of committing murder. So, I will make it easy for you. I did not kill Myles Brentwood. He came into my shop around four forty-five p.m. as he's done every Friday afternoon for as long as I can remember. He bought a small painting, no different from what he's done the last Friday of every month, we made small talk, then he left saying he had a faculty meeting to get to. That's it. Besides, why would I kill him? I adored him. He was one of the few people around here who fully appreciated fine art. I loved discussing it with him."

"I know. We all loved him. It's quite a shock if I'm honest."

"I don't understand, Ewan. Why do you think I had anything to do with this then?"

He reached out and took hold of her arm.

"I'm sorry, okay? I know you couldn't do this. I don't know what I was thinking. It's just, I have to go by the book on this one or I'll risk losing my pips. I already have my chief inspector up in my face about this case. Something like this could be blown out of proportion quickly if the papers were to get hold of it. And bad publicity is the last thing this town needs."

He grabbed hold of her other arm, tilted his head to one side, and pinned his eyes on hers from beneath his dark, raised eyebrows.

"Forgive me?" he begged.

Her anger melted easily.

"On one condition."

"Name it."

"You tell me what you know."

"I can't discuss the case, Jorgie, you must know that."

Her eyes told him he had no choice.

"Fine, but it stays between us, okay? And you promise me you won't jump to any conclusions," he agreed, strong-armed by his sudden onset of guilt over upsetting her.

"Deal."

"Myles never made it to the faculty meeting yesterday. It was due to start at five. He is never late and he has never missed a meeting either. That's what raised concern. They tried ringing him on his cell, but the thing went straight to voicemail."

"That's not really that strange for Myles. He never remembered to charge his phone."

"Right, except, Mrs. Reeves says she knows his battery was fully charged because he had asked her to charge it in her office during school and gave it to him before he left to go to your shop. So, she went past his house around six thirty on her way home, after the faculty meeting. He wasn't there either. That's when she rang us. We searched all night and finally found his body at the start of the woodland path behind your house."

He paused to see her reaction but Jorja's face didn't reveal the thoughts that suddenly flooded her mind. Perhaps Vincent's behavior was in response to something he had heard outside. Cats sense danger long before humans do.

"There's more though, Jorgie." Ewan straightened his shoulders before he spoke.

"There was a piece of art, placed on top of his body. It looked to have been crafted by hand, from copper, like the pipes you find in a house's plumbing. It's quite unique and beautiful, and without a doubt made with skill by a very talented artist. Jorgie, it was a single long-stemmed rose. We believe it was also the murder weapon."

CHAPTER THREE

Ewan's words rang in her ears. On the outside, Jorja's face told him his last piece of information had no effect on her. A skill she had learned a long time ago when her job placed her in pressured situations—or when she needed to hide from the world. For reasons she didn't quite understand her body suddenly felt necessary to draw on it, triggered into motion, and she could not stop it. It had been years since she last felt the need to withdraw. Inside, her body was once again at war with itself. It was so easy for her mind to slip back into the past. Instinctively she knew she needed to be on guard, even around her best friend, possibly especially around Ewan.

"Jorgie, say something. I told you not to jump to any conclusions. I knew I shouldn't have told you anything." He backed away and swept his hand through his thick dark-brown hair.

"I'm fine, Ewan, and I'm glad you told me. I can see why you would come knocking on my door for answers. But just because he was found dead near my house and my last name is Rose does not mean anything. I didn't kill him. I could never do that."

Her voice was aloof, almost steely. Not because she felt hurt or offended by Ewan suspecting that she was capable of murder, but because she suddenly knew why Myles Brentwood was killed. Challenging the tall stranger had proved to be a huge mistake.

"I know you didn't do it, Jorgie. Like I said, my hand is forced on this one. I want to stay on this case, catch the guy who did this, keep this town safe. And to do that I have to pull out the rulebook. So... I am going to need to ask you to come down to the station and make an official statement. So we can rule you out. Once forensics give us an approximate time of death, it will be easier to rule you out. For all we know it happened while you were at Ann's. Then you'll have an alibi."

"And if it didn't? What if it happened last night while I was sleeping, alone, with no alibi?"

"We'll cross that bridge when we get to it, if we get to it, okay? Come on. Jump in. I've got your back. Best to do this quickly before McGuthrey gets wind of it. He's been praying for a juicy story to give him that big break that will finally land him his dream job at the *Daily Mail*."

. . .

BUT IT WAS ALREADY TOO LATE. St. Ives was too small for something this big to stay a secret. When they arrived at the St. Ives police station, McGuthrey was already standing on the front steps, camera in hand.

"Unbelievable," Ewan said as he parked his car.

Jorja didn't react.

"It's fine, nothing to worry about. You and I have been friends for donkey's years. This will not be the first time we arrive at the station together. If he asks why you are here, you don't tell him anything, okay. Let's not create any sparks that could cause him to turn it into an inferno. I'll handle it."

Jorja nodded and followed Ewan from the parking lot toward the steps of the main entrance.

McGuthrey didn't waste any time and rushed toward them.

"Reid, do you know who killed Myles Brentwood? How was he killed? Any suspects?"

"Back off, McGuthrey, we don't know anything yet."

"What's the significance of the rose? There's blood on it. Is it his? Is it the murder weapon?"

"I said, back off, McGuthrey. And you shouldn't be going anywhere near the crime scene. You'll contaminate it, might even drop your DNA there, and then we'll link *you* to the murder."

Ewan's disguised warning gave the eager journalist some pause, but not enough to sway him from pushing his inquiry further.

"Why are you here, Jorja? Are you a suspect?"

"Don't fall for his tricks," Ewan whispered close to Jorja's ear as he gently ushered her toward the door.

She looked back at McGuthrey and flashed him a small smile in amusement.

"That's ridiculous, McGuthrey. I'm here to discuss the security for the upcoming art fair, that's all. Why don't you let Ewan do his job and go take some photos of the bowling club's tenth anniversary instead before I tell your mother you bought another nude sketch from me?"

Her comment sent a flush to the eager reporter's twenty-eight-year-old face and immediately had him back off.

"If you know anything, Reid, I'm the first to know, deal?" he shouted back at Ewan whose wide grin soon broke into laughter.

"Now who knows everything, huh?" he joked as they stepped inside the police station and the door shut behind them.

"The boy had it coming. He's obsessed with nudes. Someone ought to find him a wife before his sins catch up with him."

"Yeah well, perhaps he's holding out for the London girls. Anyway, let's get the ball rolling and get you out of here before Major Crimes get here. I just want to quickly make a phone call. Charlie should not have let anyone near that crime scene yet. Help yourself to some coffee, I'll be quick."

She watched Ewan step into his office to make the call. The station was quiet—most likely because he had all his constables guarding the crime scene. It seemed as if they were there alone.

St. Ives police station was much smaller than those in the larger nearby towns, equipped with just enough officers to service general police incidents. Ewan had started there as a police constable and gradually worked his way up the ranks to detective inspector, the most senior at the station and trained to handle criminal investigations of this kind. But, since murder investigations hardly, if not ever, occurred in their town, it was evident he was anxious not to botch the investigation.

She watched him through the window of his office as he impressed upon his officers at the scene to step up their game. Next to the coffee station, the printer suddenly whirred, startling her into almost spilling her fresh mug of coffee. She fixed her eyes on the machine as it started processing a sheet of paper. Before long it spat out a color copy of Myles Brentwood's bloody body, lying sprawled on his back across the forest path behind her house. She drew in a sharp breath, caught off guard by the next photo that dropped into the printing tray atop the first. His head was covered in blood, his eyes wide and filled with angst, as if he had been frightened when he died and frozen in place.

The next photo delivered a close-up of his neck and a large puncture wound to one side; his left side. Jorja's heart pounded in her chest as she took in the brutality of the crime. She was simultaneously repulsed and overcome with fear. Before long, the printer ejected another printed copy, this time one of the rose that was made entirely from copper. Ewan was right. It was unique and an awe-inspiring piece of art. But her admiration soon turned to disgust as the next photo had zoomed in to the tip of the stem that was covered in blood. Suddenly panic engulfed her as she realized how Myles had died. She slammed her mug onto the table, spilling half of its contents across the coffee tray. She spun around and bolted toward the exit. Her pace quickened and she bumped her hips against the corners of several desks along the way in a desperate attempt to run out of the station.

"Hey, Jorgie. Wait! What's wrong?" Ewan yelled from behind his desk, slamming the phone's receiver down on the desk as he rushed toward her. But she had already found the front door and started running down the steps. In her wake, she heard Ewan running after her, shouting for her to stop. She couldn't. She had to get out of there. Had to run, as fast as she could.

Overcome by emotions she couldn't quite make sense of yet, she ran toward her house, glancing over her shoulder every few strides. Conscious of feeling exposed, she pulled her hoodie over her head, grateful she had decided to wear it that morning instead of her usual neon reflective jacket. She took the cobbled path that led away from the center of town toward the beach. She would zigzag through the fishermen's cottages and cross the stretch of bluff to where it met up with the other side of the woodland that bordered her house. Once she reached it she would stay clear of the path and find a way through the dense trees, avoiding the crime scene. She had been in those woods a thousand times and knew her way through the trees. With Major Crimes still en route, there would be no more than the four constables that were on duty at any given time during the week, eight at the most if Ewan had called in the rest of his unit who were off duty. With any luck, they would all be guarding the immediate perimeter of the crime scene, which should leave her path clear to slip in through the side entrance of her house. Ewan would most certainly come looking for her there first, but she would lock herself in, for now. She needed time to think, time to collect herself. Time to process. Alone, just her, the real her.

CHAPTER FOUR

Panic flooded her veins as she navigated her way through the dense woods behind her house. She had slowed to a brisk walk, proceeding with the utmost caution to avoid bumping into any of the neighbors who regularly walked their dogs there. The crisp scent of fresh foliage that had always brought her such peace now acted as a detecting system. She filled her nostrils, relying on her senses to detect danger. Though she was as light-footed as a gazelle, her presence scared a few squirrels that were feverishly scouring the ground to gather the last of what the season offered before the cold set in. Nearby, she heard a rustle in the bushes behind her and looked back. The dense foliage made it difficult to see anything so she bent at the waist to have a proper look. When she didn't see anything, she brushed it off as another squirrel, or perhaps a fox. Off the footpath, it was hard to move through the thicket and it slowed her down. Her route there was shorter than if she had run along the road, but even so, she was running out of time to get home before Ewan got there. She picked up her pace, hooking her bare legs on the spiky leaves of the nettle patches. As she neared her house, she could hear Charlie's voice drifting in the breeze toward her. She crouched down behind a tree, peering around it to see if she was visible to him and the squad. They were searching in the undergrowth around the body, engrossed in their task. Determining she was out of their view, she changed direction and zigzagged from tree to tree until she was within ten yards of her house. With her side door in full view, she paused behind a tree, assessing if any constables were patrolling her house. The coast was clear.

She drew a deep breath, exhaled, and darted across the narrow strip of lawn toward the door. Her long limbs ensured she did it in only three strides before her feet leaped the two steps up to the door.

As always, her door was unlocked—quite common for people living in St. Ives. She shut the door behind her, bolted the latch at the top, then the key in the door. She paused briefly, her back to the door, scanning her eyes through the cozy kitchen. Everything seemed exactly as she had left it earlier that morning. When she didn't hear any sounds coming from the rest of the house, she moved through the kitchen and down the small corridor to lock the front door. Her fingers moved quickly, first the latch at the top, then the key. Her body tingled with adrenaline. She had made it home unnoticed.

As the endorphins slowly dissipated and her brain kicked into clarity, she made her way back to the kitchen and gulped down a small bottle of water from the fridge. Her eye caught a magnet she had gotten as a birthday gift the previous year. Ewan had given it to her. It was a four-by-four-inch picture of a waterfall running into a beautiful pond. A biblical scripture was written across it. She allowed herself to take it in.

The Lord is my shepherd, I shall not be in want.
He makes me lie down in green pastures,
He leads me beside quiet waters,
He restores my soul.

She waited for the words to mean something, anything. But nothing happened. It rang empty, devoid of any emotion. She never really got why he gave it to her in the first place and always thought it must have had some special meaning to him since he was more committed to their faith than she was. So, she left it on her fridge door as a sign of respect—or to trick him into thinking that it had meant something to her too. He had tried to get her to attend church more regularly, but for some reason, she couldn't. It made her feel vulnerable—a place where someone bigger than her knew her deepest, darkest secrets. She went when she felt like it—which was all of perhaps once a month to appease Ewan and keep up her facade. It wasn't that she did not believe that there was a God, she did. She just wasn't ready to let go of who she used to be and so desperately yearned to one day be again. Letting the community—and Ewan—believe she had already crossed the line of faith made living there easier somehow—not to mention ensured her cover. The reminder of her past jolted her into the present and she dropped the empty water bottle into the recycling. Her shoes squeaked on the tiled floor as she started pacing the small space in her kitchen. *Think Jorja, think!* She swept her medium-length blonde hair back and tucked it behind her ears, locking her hands in the nape of her neck to help her focus.

Her mind wandered to the man who'd stood across the street. She hadn't liked the look of him then and most certainly now had the eerie feeling that he'd had a hand in Myles' demise. As her memory played back his last moments in her shop she shut her eyes in an attempt to recall any details about the man she might have over-looked. But her mind was foggy. Instead, the heavy feeling of dread that had been simmering in the pit of her stomach slowly pushed up and settled in her chest. She threw her head back and drew in several deep breaths to encourage her body to get rid of it, but it didn't. Panic set in.

She tried to calm her thoughts, reasoning that she should have just told Ewan about him, let him handle it, and do what he was trained to do. But something had held her back from mentioning the man to him. Perhaps it was because she refused to believe it was possible, tried to convince herself that there was no way on earth they could have known where she was. That they could not have finally found her.

But in the very depths of her gut, hidden behind the heavy feeling in her chest, she knew her instincts were on point. She had wronged many people in her life, too many to count. Even her parents when she left home that day and spat angered words at them. But there were only ever two enemies of whom she needed to be afraid. And both had just cause and the means to take their revenge.

Propelled by the notion that Myles' murder might very well have been a message of warning to her, she charged out of the kitchen and up into her bedroom. Her mind and body seemed to have taken on a will of their own as she yanked open her closet doors and shoved a rack of clothing to one side. On the floor of her wardrobe stood a small drawer unit and she fought to drag it over to one side. It was heavier than she recalled it being, not having needed to move it since she arrived almost twenty years earlier. She panted as it finally gave way under her strength and she dropped to her knees in front of the space it had occupied. Her fingers moved quickly to pull up one of the corners of the carpet where it had been sliced into a neat square flap. Beneath it, the wooden floor lay exposed and she reached into one of the drawers of the unit to retrieve a flat tool—similar to one a sculptor would use to carve clay. She wedged the flat point between the floorboards. One easily lifted away and she moved to lift the other. Her hand reached down and from the dark corners beneath the floorboards, she retrieved a small duffle bag. The black leather was covered in a thick layer of dust that puffed into a small cloud as she dropped it on the floor beside her. Panic made way for hesitation when she reached for the zipper. Never, after all this time, having remained hidden in the safe confines of St. Ives at the furthermost point of England, did she ever think she'd have to face either of them again. The notion gave her chills, knowing that either of them, if not both, was quite capable of killing her. And why wouldn't they? She had destroyed one's life and robbed from the other.

A lonely tear threatened to run down her cheek. She had come to love her life in St. Ives, and all the people who welcomed her. The last words Myles had said to her were that she was the best thing that had ever happened to them, a blessing. Now, it seemed as if she was the direct opposite. She has cursed this town, brought with her the sins of her past. A past the residents of St. Ives were now paying dearly for.

She vigorously wiped away the tear that had settled on her chin then her fingers moved to pull back the zipper.

And as she pulled back her shoulders, resolved to doing what she needed to do to protect the town—and Ewan— she emptied the contents of the bag onto the soft carpet next to her.

CHAPTER FIVE

E wan disappeared back into the police station and stood staring at the space where Jorja had waited for him. His hands pushed the panels of his suit jacket back before they settled on his hips. Something had unnerved her, made her run, made her retreat into her shell. Something had triggered her to run out of the station. He had fought for years to gain her trust but always sensed she was holding out on him. Not even when they tried taking their friendship further did she fully open up to him, and he knew she wanted to, was desperate to surrender all she held cooped up inside. It was as if she couldn't. As if trusting someone would penetrate the protective wall she had built around her.

He walked over to the coffee station; saw where she had spilled half her mug of coffee.

A voice behind him startled him.

"Ah, there you are, sir." PC Bennett had come in from the file room and moved to a desk directly behind Ewan.

"Sorry, didn't mean to scare you, sir." The young police constable dropped a Manila folder on his desk and waited for his superior to respond. When he didn't, he continued talking.

"The first of the crime scene photos came in; they should be there on the printer," he pushed his chin toward the machine next to Ewan. "I've just opened the case file so will start recording what we know so far."

Ewan's eyes lingered on the photos in the machine and instantly knew that was what had scared Jorja. She must have seen them. He snatched the photos from the printing tray, briefly scanned each one, and then handed them to his constable.

"Thanks, make sure no one sees them, Bennett. We cannot leave these things lying around. This is a murder investigation, not a pub brawl."

"Yes, sir, sorry, sir."

Ewan charged into his office, snatched his car keys and cell phone from the desk, then made his way to the exit.

"And make sure every single piece of evidence that comes in is under lock and key, got it?" he shouted over his shoulder as he rushed out.

ONCE HE REACHED Jorja's house, he parked the car in her driveway then briefly walked round the back of the house to check in with his squad who were still working the crime scene.

"Anything new?" he asked his sergeant, Charlie.

"Not yet, sir. The men are combing the area for evidence, and we're still waiting for forensics to arrive, but we should get a time of death any second now." His eyebrows lifted as his eyes pointed to where the coroner had just inserted a spike into the body.

Ewan stepped closer to the victim's body and waited for the announcement. *Please Lord: let it be when she was at Ann's.*

"Time of death between midnight and four this morning. Cause of death: a puncture wound to the carotid artery. Most likely from this copper rose. The victim was killed somewhere else then brought here to be discovered. He would have bled out in minutes. There is not enough blood here for this to be where the victim was killed. I'll know more once I examine the body, but I am pretty sure he was brought here."

Ewan rotated in place, scanning the immediate perimeter.

"I don't see any tire tracks."

"Exactly, he was carried here, most likely over someone's shoulder judging by these postmortem bruises that are starting to set in across his abdomen. I would guess about sixty to ninety minutes after he was killed. But, as I said, I'll know more once I inspect the rest of his body."

"Thanks, please keep me posted," Ewan said and turned to Charlie.

"Send two men to Myles' house to check it out. It might have happened there. Be alert and do not touch anything. Record everything, got it?"

"Copy that, sir."

Ewan turned and walked toward Jorja's house. From the outside, it seemed she was not there. The shutters and curtains were closed. When he reached her front door, he briefly turned to inspect the area behind him, then gently knocked on the door.

JORJA FOUND her mind and body had entered into a state of complete calm as she emptied the contents of the bag onto the floor. It was as if her mind had switched to stealth mode—calm and controlled. Panic and fear had left her and instead, invited laser-sharp focus in their place.

She picked up three bundles of cash, each in a different currency—US dollars, Swiss francs, and Russian rubles. She pushed them to one side and picked up three passports, each matching the country origins of the money. She flipped the first one open with her thumb—United States—and stared down at the picture of the brown-haired woman with black-framed glasses. It was under a different name. She set it down on the carpet and proceeded to the next passport. This time she had long ash-brown hair and bright red lipstick—her Swiss identity. She reached for the last travel document, hesitating as a sudden jolt of nerves hit the pit of her stomach. She thumbed back the cover and took in the photo of the woman with bright red hair that was cropped into spikes atop her head. This was who she'd been when it all happened, when she had risked everything. She looked up at the black leather jacket that hung in the back of her closet—the one she had worn at the time the photo was taken. The one she had always worn back then. She caught a glimpse of herself in the mirror that was stuck to the inside of the closet door next to her and allowed her eyes to linger over her face. She didn't look anything like any of these women anymore. For one, she had aged at least twenty years, and for another, she had grown her hair out to its natural medium blonde, trimmed into a sophisti-cated short style that curled in the nape of her neck. Even she would not recognize her now.

Her attention went back to the contents of the bag, as she dropped the Russian passport on top of the others. There were a set of suction pads, a bottle of talcum powder, a stethoscope, two mobile phones, a pager, and a gun—a SIG Sauer P226 semi-automatic pistol. She moved to pick it up, surprised at the flood of excitement that rushed through her veins when her hand closed around the cold steel grip. With experienced precision, she pulled back the slide release with her other hand to reveal that the chamber was empty. Her thumb moved to eject the full cartridge, briefly checking it before she clipped it back into place, and flicked on the safety.

Interrupted by a knock at her front door, her mind snapped back to the present. She stayed seated on the floor, frozen, listening. The knocking grew louder, this time accompanied by Ewan's voice calling out her name. She knew she couldn't ignore him; he was not one to easily give up.

She gathered the items on the floor and scooped them back inside the leather bag. Everything, except the gun, which she pushed to one side while she hastily dropped the bag back into its place under the floor. Ewan knocked again and she moved quickly to hide the gun under her pillow before racing down the staircase to open the door.

Ewan's eyes darted over and around her shoulders when she opened the door to let him in, checking that she wasn't in any danger.

"I'm alone, Ewan." She turned and started toward her kitchen. He followed.

"Is that it? You are just going to pretend nothing is going on here?" he said as he stood in the entrance to the kitchen while she put on the kettle.

"I don't know what you want me to say, Ewan."

"Well, for a start, why did you run? I told you I needed a statement, but you just upped and left. What's going on, Jorgie?"

She walked to the fridge to grab the milk, bringing it to her nose to sniff if it was fresh. From the kitty door behind them, Vincent made himself known and she poured a few drops of milk into his saucer on the floor.

"Jorgie, please don't ignore me. What's going on? I assume you saw the photos in the printer. You should not have seen them, but still, was it enough to cause you to run off like that?"

"Sorry, it upset me, but I'm fine now." The tone of her voice was unapproachable.

Ewan shook his head as he moved closer to where she had busied herself with the teabags and stood with her back toward him.

"Yeah well, I'm not fine. I have never pushed you to share anything you might not be comfortable sharing. All these years, Jorgie, I have given you space, proved you could trust me. Heck, even when you put the brakes on our relationship I let it go. But I know you, Jorja Rose. You withdraw when things get too close for comfort for you, too close to what brought you to St. Ives all those years ago. Why? What about Myles Brentwood's murder is making you crawl into your shell, huh? What are you not telling me?"

CHAPTER SIX

E wan waited, praying she would let him inside her invisible fortress, but instead, she continued making the tea and remained standing with her back toward him.

Ewan softened his tone.

"I know you didn't kill Myles, Jorgie. You couldn't have. He was killed somewhere else and his body was moved here. There's no way you could have picked him up and carried him into that forest, and we know he was carried in because there are no drag marks or tire tracks in the ground anywhere around him."

Again, he waited for her to respond. The new information had brought her some relief. Enough to instantly decide that there was no reason for her to run, at least not yet. She would be on her guard, be careful, wait a little while longer, make sure it was just a random murder that had nothing to do with her past.

She turned to face him.

"So, you believe me now?"

"I never said I didn't believe you, Jorgie. I know you didn't kill him. I just needed your statement, to line it up so no one can point a finger at you."

He moved closer to her, placed his hands on her elbows, and forced her to make eye contact with him.

"Have I ever given you any reason not to trust me, Jorgie? I know you know more than you are telling me. Let me in. I'm on your side, heck I have always been on your side. Whatever battle you're fighting in that pretty head of yours, you don't have to fight alone." He could have continued to tell her God was there too and that the battle was His, but he didn't. He held back.

Ewan's eyes held hers captive, the jade color suddenly looking as alluring as an island ocean. Ewan Reid was a handsome man, and she had never denied that there was a spark between them. She wanted to surrender. Show him who she really was, tell him everything, and accept his help. But she couldn't. Ewan Reid was a man of principle and he wouldn't look at her the same way ever again if he knew who she really was and what she had done before she came to St. Ives. Besides, she had learned a long time ago that no one could be trusted, ever. No one but herself. Letting her guard down now would be a mistake. A mistake their friendship might never recover from not to mention that his life would be at risk, possibly now more than ever.

"I don't know what you're talking about, Ewan. I'm fine, honestly. I shouldn't have looked at the photos. It isn't exactly something I see every day and just caught me off guard, that's all."

She turned to finish making the tea.

"If you ever need to get something off your chest I'm here for you. God is too."

She laughed as she handed him his cup of tea.

"Oh, I very much doubt God would want to help me, trust me. He will take one look at me and walk on by. Not everyone is as holy as you, Ewan."

"Holy? I am far from it, Jorgie. The only things in my life that are holy are my socks."

He waited for his quip to soften her edges. She smiled over the brim of her cup and rolled her eyes at his cheesy humor.

"Great, I have a smile. Now, can I please ask you to pop by the station later to give us that formal statement? I cannot put a foot wrong on this investigation, Jorgie, so I need your cooperation, okay? I'm asking as a friend." His warm friendly eyes pinned hers down again.

"Fine, I'll pop by after I get cleaned up. Speaking of which, how long is he going to lie there?"

"Who?"

"Myles, who else? I can see him from my bedroom window and it's disturbing."

Her words held Ewan's attention as he digested her revelation.

"You can see him from your bedroom window," he repeated.

"Yes, I just said that."

Ewan set his cup down on the nearby counter, turned, and charged upstairs to her window.

"What are you doing? You can't just run into my bedroom."

She had not said that out of modesty, rather concern for him discovering her gun under her pillow. She followed him into her bedroom and found him already standing in front of her window.

She was right, he thought. She could see everything from up there, in great detail.

He turned to face her again, his eyebrows drawn into a frown.

"You didn't hear anything last night? Nothing at all?"

"No, I was sound asleep."

She decided to tell him about Vincent.

"Except—"

"Except what, Jorgie?"

"Well, Vincent seemed to have been disturbed by something in the house."

"What time was that?"

"Around four thirty, I think."

"And you're only telling me this now."

"Yes, I didn't make anything of it at the time, he's a cat. I thought he was just full of beans. But thinking about it now he did seem frightened. He crawled under the spare bed and bolted for the bushes when I left to go on my run."

Ewan was deep in thought as he took it all in.

"Do you think Vincent heard the murderer?"

Ewan turned to look at her, ignoring her question, his eyes suddenly serious.

"How certain are you that there was no one else inside your house when you got up this morning?"

The weight of his question hit her square in the thorax, her face declaring the angst that suddenly engulfed her.

"I-no-I don't know. Why?"

"You said Vincent got scared and ran to hide in the bushes the moment you opened the door. He would not have bolted from the house to hide outside if the danger was out there waiting for him. He would have done the exact opposite if something, or someone, spooked him and the threat was outside. He would have stayed indoors, under the bed, where he was safe."

"You think the guy who murdered Myles was inside my house. While I was asleep? While I got ready for my run?"

"It certainly is possible, and it won't hurt to be sure. I'm going to get a few lads to dust for fingerprints." He was already on his cell phone.

"When, now?" Her eyes darted to her pillow, then her cupboard, noting her door that had sprung open and stood slightly ajar. She had packed her bag in such a hurry that she was now not sure the set of drawers lined up properly with where its weight had left indentations in the carpet and fully concealed the sliced flap.

"Yes, now. Every minute that goes by is one minute closer to the killer disappearing. If my hunch is correct, he was inside your house, Jorgie. Why, I don't know yet, but I can't ignore the notion."

She watched as he peered through the curtain while talking on his cell to his team outside. If they find the duffle bag, or worse, the gun, she would have a lot more to explain.

"Okay, well could I have a few minutes just to freshen up before they come in, please? I'm still a bit sweaty from my run this morning."

Ewan's eyes swept across the room and settled on her en suite bathroom.

"Sure, just make it quick, and try not to touch or disrupt anything too much. I'll have the men start on the doors and windows downstairs."

He turned and left the room, shutting her bedroom door behind him.

When she was alone in her room she leaped to her closet and checked that she had placed the drawer unit back in position, she hadn't—they would have certainly noticed the deep lines in the carpet that revealed where it had been cut. At first, she thought she would just move it back, but then decided it was best she hide the gun back under the floor too. She heard Ewan's voice downstairs as he let his men in. She would have to hurry. Abandoning the closet, she ran to turn on the shower and then moved to retrieve the gun from beneath her pillow. Ewan's voice trailed his footsteps on the stairs. Her heart pounded in her chest, yet she remained in control of her body. She skittered across to the bed, retrieved her pistol, then glided toward her closet.

A knock sounded on her bedroom door and Ewan's voice announced he was on the other side of it.

Her hands paused over the loose floorboards, careful not to make a sound.

"Jorgie, I've got the lads at it downstairs. I'll catch up with you later, forensics have finally arrived."

"Sure, thanks," she yelled back and waited until she heard the wooden stairs groan under his feet as he went downstairs. Her hands moved quickly, lifting the floorboards then hiding her gun in the leather duffle bag. Once she'd moved the drawer unit back into place, she pulled her clothes over the rail, closing the gaps around the unit so everything appeared undisturbed.

Everything but the dark secrets of her past that now threatened to bubble up to the surface and disrupt everything she had worked so hard to keep hidden.

CHAPTER SEVEN

In the days that followed the gruesome murder that had the entire seaside town on edge, the once tranquil atmosphere had shifted into rumbling gossip, fear, and general unease. The crime had taken the town by surprise and to add insult to their holiday-safe reputation, every fame-seeking reporter in Cornwall had come down in the hopes of scooping the story. But, as with these small seaside towns, the residents stood firm, protecting their territory like an animal during breeding season. They had formed small civil policing groups that took shifts guarding the two entrances into town, the shops in the village, and in and around the small residential neighborhood—a welcome relief to the understaffed police station who had their hands full with the investigation.

With the annual St. Ives art fair approaching, and all her usual help occupied with guarding their town, Jorja kept to herself. She worked tirelessly in the hopes of settling her own unease that seemed to tighten its grip on her heart with each day that passed. Grateful for the art fair to distract her, she buried her anxiety in the preparations, spending more than one night working late in her gallery. In a desperate effort to rid her body from the gut feeling that gnawed at the insides of her stomach, she told herself that she was imagining danger, that Myles Brentwood's death had nothing to do with her, and that she was safe.

Having pulled every resource available to them, the police were no closer to catching the perpetrator responsible for the evil deed. It was as if all leads died on the leafy forest floor, where Myles' body was found. Major Crimes had stepped in and taken over the investigation, leaving Ewan to run around like a puppy on a leash. He had texted her a few times to let her know that he would pop in to check on her as soon as he could, but it had been four days since they last saw or spoke to each other.

She glanced at her wristwatch. It was an hour before midnight. Outside her small gallery, the street was dark and deserted. She hadn't realized the time and resolved to head home, grateful the threatening weather had prompted her to come to work in her car that morning instead of by foot as she normally did. She closed the folder she had been poring over on the antique desk that stood in the rear of her shop, reached for her cup, and lifted it to gulp down the last few mouthfuls of now-cold tea. As she brought the lip of her teacup to her mouth the light from the nearby desk lamp reflected off the narrow gold band that ran around the inside rim of the cup, exposing a dark shadow directly behind her. She knew in that very instant she was not alone and spun around to see who it was but it was too late.

Her head was violently pulled back against someone's hard body, held in place by something around her neck. Black-gloved hands on either side of her head yanked back harder, restricting the airflow through her windpipe.

She gasped.

Gagged.

Fought for air.

As the last of the oxygen in her lungs ran out, her fingers scrabbled to loosen whatever was around her neck.

It couldn't.

In a final desperate attempt to have her attacker relax his grip to let the life back into her lungs, she reached back and snatched at the intruder's face. Her fingers searched for his eyes, the tips sensing rough stubble instead.

He pulled back harder.

She felt her head compress, her eyes bulging under the pressure.

Survival instincts kicked in.

Her legs extended, pushing into the parquet floor under her feet. Her body heaved back, knocking the Windsor chair over in the process. She pushed her legs down harder, drove her heels into the floor, and forced the attacker's weight to shift. The noose around her neck slackened, just enough to allow a little bit of air into her lungs and smell the alcohol on his breath.

Two of her fingers found their way in between her flesh and the rubbery wire around her neck. He regained his balance, pulling back on the wire again.

It sliced into the soft flesh of her fingers.

She fought hard not to faint. Nearly did so twice.

He groaned.

She fought back. But he was too strong. The energy slowly drained from her body and she could feel her life slowly slipping away.

Her feet left the floor, and her legs and body felt heavy, straining against the restraint blocking her airways.

She reached for the desk lamp with her free arm but it was too far away.

Her fingers searched blindly, snatching at anything that might aid her in her fight to survive.

It was futile.

She caught herself asking God to help her. She had never done that before for fear of God rejecting her, but it was all she had left.

A tear escaped down her cheek, made her feel vulnerable. She hated the feeling, hated herself for being afraid.

From somewhere behind there was a shuffle on the wooden floor, then another male voice. The wire around her neck relaxed and she drew an involuntary breath as she flopped to the floor, pulling the cord of the lamp with her. The lamp smashed and shattered into pieces on the floor next to her.

The room was plunged into near darkness. She gasped and blinked several times to force her eyes to regain focus in the dark room. Behind her, groans echoed through the small space then, what sounded like a chair breaking. She crawled across the floor, feeling the impact of someone falling onto the floor next to her leg. She flinched, her mind suddenly clear on what was happening.

As she flung her body around and pushed herself further away from the commotion, she regained all her senses. Her eyes traced the silhouettes of two men as they wrestled on the floor. One was entirely clothed in black, the other in a light gray suit. *Ewan!*

The intruder was on top of him, holding him down with one arm while the other drew back and drove a fist into Ewan's jaw.

She tried screaming for him to stop as she scrambled to her feet, but her throat had not fully recovered yet.

The sudden change in posture made her dizzy and she froze in place for a few seconds. Just enough to see her attacker deliver several more blows to Ewan's face. The man rose to his feet, stretching tall above her and watching him from behind, his height instantly revealed his similarity to the man who'd stood across the street. She watched as he pulled a wire from a strap around his left wrist, then bent forward to put it around Ewan's neck.

It was as if every reflex in her body jerked into action

and her mind instantly recalled the tactics she'd thought had long since left her.

Her foot smashed into her assailant's back, causing him to tumble to the floor. He was quick to his feet immediately towering over her once more. Her hands were up in front of her face, palms stretched out and facing each other, prepared for his attack.

He thrust his fist forward. She ducked to the left. Once again he punched the air in front of her face, she ducked the other way, then thrust her flat hand into his chest. It rendered him off balance and gasping for air. Her body flexed, she pivoted, then extended one leg high above her waist, whipping her foot across his jaw.

The impact thrust him against the wall and he slumped to the floor.

Next to her, Ewan moaned and she turned to look. It was no more than a second. Something hard hit her legs, forcing her to her knees. Before she knew it, the man's arm had her in a chokehold. He was strong, stronger than before. Propelled by hatred, intentionally wanting to bring her harm. Kill her.

Ewan coughed and tried to get up. His mouth was covered in blood, so was his right eye. He looked up and spotted Jorja in trouble. His body was weak, too weak to get up.

His eyes locked with Jorja's. Fear lay deep in both their eyes. He reached for his gun. His holster was empty. He looked back; saw the smugness in the attacker's eyes. Moments later he stared down the barrel of his own gun.

It was as if time had stood still in the moments that ensued. Still immobilized by the man's grip around her neck, Jorja saw the intruder's other arm extend past the side of her face. As it did so, his sleeve brushed against her cheek before he pointed the gun at Ewan. Fear made way for anger and she let go of the elbow she had tried to pull away from her neck. Her fingers wrapped around his wrist, twisting his arm, and twisting her body along with it, until the gunman's arm was contorted upside down.

The strain on his armpit made him cry out in pain. Several oaths escaped from his mouth, then, out of nowhere, his bald head slammed hard against her forehead leaving her breathless as she stumbled a few paces back on her feet.

He turned the gun on her, pointing it directly at her face. She watched his index finger tighten around the trigger, expecting the bullet to banish her to hell, accepting that she probably deserved it.

Then suddenly Ewan's face came into view, his body wedged between her and the gun.

The gun went off.

Ewan's full weight was on top of her and she found herself pinned between him and the floor, moments before darkness blotted out all light and sound around them.

CHAPTER EIGHT

She had no idea how long she had been lying on the floor but by the time Jorja opened her eyes, the moon was high. She could tell from how it beamed its silver light to a spot on the bottom of the wall next to her. Her head hurt and she let out a soft moan. The space around her slowly came into focus. In the moonlit room, her eyes traced the shadowy half-circles of the fish scale ceiling above her. She was flat on her back, head in the doorway that opened to the front of her gallery. She knew because she had brought in a freelance contractor from London to add the texture technique to her ceiling.

She tried moving her body but couldn't. Something was on top of her, weighing her down. Her mind scrambled to figure it out, recalling the events that had brought her there. It took only a few seconds to remember what had happened.

"Ewan," she whispered, realizing he was still on top of her.

He wasn't answering, or moving.

Her hand went to shake his shoulder. He didn't stir so she called out for him again, wriggling her body beneath him as she tried to free herself. But it was no use. He wasn't moving, nor could she get out from under him.

Suddenly realizing their attacker might still be around she froze, scanning the area as best she could. There was nothing but dead silence. Assuming he had left them both for dead she managed to get one hand to the side of Ewan's neck—there was a pulse, faint but a heartbeat, nonetheless.

"Ewan," she called out again.

Still he did not answer.

Her hand lowered to his torso where she aimed to drag him off by grabbing hold of his jacket. Something felt sticky. She let her hand blindly search for the source, tracing the sticky moisture to where her fingers soon disappeared in a shallow pool just below his left shoulder. It took a split second for her to realize it was blood and that he had been shot.

Shot by the bullet that was intended for her. He had saved her life.

Adrenaline rushed through her body and forced its way into her arms all while she continued to call him back to consciousness. It was only when she pulled her leg up to wedge her knee under his hips that his body rolled off and plonked onto the floor next to her. It took no time at all for her to get up and hover over his body, staring down at the open wound in his shoulder.

"Ewan, can you hear me? Wake up!" she patted his cheek, each time with more vigor until the quietest of moans escaped from his lips.

Her hands pushed down on the pool of blood that had started to well up under his jacket.

"It's okay, you're going to be okay. Stay with me, Ewan."

He moaned again.

She vaulted to the phone that lay upside down on the floor beneath her desk, pulling the cord to free the receiver that had landed inside the wastepaper basket.

Her bloody fingers dialed for an ambulance, barely aware of the words she spoke when they answered. Her attention was with Ewan who had since opened his eyes and was desperate to say something.

She pinched the phone between her shoulder and ear and knelt beside him. His eyes looked urgent while his lips moved with hardly any sound emerging from it.

The emergency operator interrupted and asked for any details she could remember about the shooter. She couldn't answer that. Should not answer her—she needed more time.

"I don't know. I can't remember, just hurry! He's lost a lot of blood, please, hurry!"

She slammed the receiver back on the cradle then

turned her full attention to Ewan whose eyes looked even more desperate to say something.

"You shouldn't talk, Ewan. They're on their way, just hold on for me, okay?"

But he ignored her, hooked his good arm's hand behind her neck, and gently pulled her ear to his mouth.

"Leave anger to God," he whispered in staccato words.

His words took her by surprise. She didn't quite know what to make of it and stared down into his eyes, the green color now suddenly dull.

"Hush, don't try to talk. You can tell me when you are better." She smiled.

Once more, he pulled her in so he could speak. This time his words came in the form of a Bible verse: Leviticus 19:18

She caressed his face.

"I'll read it, okay? Hush now, save your energy."

The ambulance sirens rang in the distance and drew closer with each passing second.

"They're almost here, Ewan. Not long now."

She jumped to her feet and darted across the small shop floor to unlock the front door, leaving it open to invite them in, then hurried back to Ewan's side to wait for the paramedics. Even in the soft moonlight, she could see Ewan's breath becoming shallow and his eyes less responsive.

"Oh no you don't, Ewan Reid! Don't you dare bail on me! Do you hear me? Stay with me, Ewan. Fight!"

She was close to panic, but didn't allow her voice to make it known to him. His eyes threatened to close and she tapped him on his cheek to wake him up. From the street she heard the ambulance pull up, followed by a police car.

"In here!" she called out to them moments before she watched Ewan close his eyes.

It was all she could do not to let anger and fear engulf her as she shouted for Ewan to open his eyes. The paramedics were already on the floor next to him and she felt someone lift her to her feet to usher her away. It was Charlie.

"Let them do their work, Jorja. It'll be okay."

They watched in horror as the paramedics worked to save Ewan's life before they rushed him out on a gurney toward the ambulance.

"I need to go with him," Jorja announced, already chasing after them as they loaded Ewan into the back of the ambulance.

"I can't allow that, ma'am, I'm sorry. His condition is critical. You are welcome to follow us." The female paramedic slammed the ambulance door shut without saying another word and Jorja watched as the vehicle sped off.

"Jump in," Charlie motioned toward his police vehicle. "I'll leave PC Daniels here to call for backup and to process the scene."

Jorja did not hesitate and quickly settled into the seat next to Charlie. When they were a fair distance away, Charlie glanced at her.

"You haven't said a word since we arrived at your gallery, Jorja. Are you sure you're not hurt?"

"Uh-huh, I'm fine. I just cannot believe what happened. I could never live with myself if Ewan—"

"Don't even think it. He is in good hands. We have to have faith that he will pull through. Besides, it wasn't your fault."

He paused briefly before he asked, "Care to tell me what happened? I mean we're going to need to take down a statement, but anything you can recall right now will help catch whoever did this."

Her body went rigid as she searched for an answer.

Charlie nudged her again.

"You're in shock, I get it, but it's really important you tell me everything you remember, Jorja. The sooner we have a lead to follow the less time the guy has to get away. Was it a burglar?"

For the briefest of moments, she thought of telling Charlie about the man across the street and her suspicions that it was he—and who it was she was now certain he worked for. But she couldn't, not yet, and certainly not to Charlie. He was too inexperienced. He would undoubtedly let it slip to his chief inspector since a breakthrough in a case of this magnitude would most certainly gain him an additional pip in rank—not to mention the threat it would pose if word got out that she was still alive.

"Was it a burglar, Jorja? Was it more than one?" He pushed again.

"I don't know. It all happened so fast," she finally answered.

"Try to remember, Jorja... anything. Why were you at the gallery so late at night? Why was Ewan with you?"

She knew Charlie was not going to let up so she told him as much as she could to shake him off her back for now.

"I was working late, alone, on the arrangements for the fair. Next thing I know, I am choked from behind. I didn't see who it was or how many there were. I must have blacked out or something when I couldn't breathe because all I remember seeing was Ewan rushing toward me. There was a gunshot and Ewan fell forward onto me. That is it. I woke up with him bleeding out on top of me and immediately called 999. That's all I can remember right now."

"That's good, a start, at least. So, let's assume they were burglars. I left Ewan at the station earlier this evening. Perhaps they tripped an alarm?"

"I don't know how, I was inside and I didn't have the alarm on. I didn't even hear him come in."

"So there was one person. You said him, not them."

"I don't know for sure. I think so."

"Okay, if it was a burglar, why did he choose to break into your gallery? Were there any paintings of value in the shop?"

She paused to think, then answered.

"No, not really, at least not anymore."

CHAPTER NINE

Charlie's eyes said it all, even in the dark confines of his car.

"What do you mean 'not anymore'?"

She hesitated briefly, then answered.

"Most of the paintings in my shop were by local artists or cheap replicas of famous paintings. But I have been helping Myles acquire a small collection of paintings by Monet. That's why he was in my shop, to collect one of the paintings in the series. I had acquired it for him through Mullers in London about a year ago—we'd arranged that he would buy one piece per month over a year. There were twelve paintings altogether. The one he'd just bought was the tenth one in Monet's Charing Cross Bridge series, painted between 1899 and 1902 when Monet spent time in London."

"And these paintings were valuable?"

"If they were originals, yes, upward of twenty-seven million dollars. But these were replicas, exceptionally good ones, but replicas, nonetheless, done by another French artist who near perfected Monet's techniques. These paintings increase in value the higher the quality of the replica. Myles paid five hundred quid for them."

"Each?" Charlie could not hide the shock in his voice.

She nodded, figuring it was okay to divulge the price her client had paid considering how Myles had died. Perhaps Charlie was onto something and she was just paranoid.

"I would imagine that, in the wrong hands, something like this could create an opportunity for fraud."

"I'm not in the business of defrauding people, Charlie."

He had touched a nerve.

"I didn't mean to insinuate that, Jorja, sorry. I just don't understand why someone would willingly pay that much money for fake paintings."

"The value lies in the pleasure of seeing a piece like that hang on your wall, Charlie, especially if it's an entire collection of one of the most famous artists of all time. Myles loved Monet's work."

Charlie suddenly fell silent.

"And you say he had intentions of buying the entire collection."

"Yes, sort of."

Charlie looked confused so she explained.

"Monet painted thirty-seven paintings in total but he

only completed twelve while living in London. This was one of the most prolific periods of Monet's career, so there is definite value in these paintings. Even replicas."

Charlie digested the art lesson then finally spoke again.

"Is it possible to mistake Myles' paintings for the real thing?"

"I suppose it is to the normal man on the street, yes, but most art collectors would have them appraised before entering into any transactions worth that kind of money."

"But to someone who doesn't know, someone who might have been told they were real, they could be sold off for twenty-seven million dollars."

Jorja felt a jolt in the pit of her stomach. Charlie's words evoked something that she had buried and hidden away for decades now.

"Anything is possible, Charlie. Why are you asking me this?" She sounded defensive. It caught her off guard. Who was she so desperate to defend, she thought, then changed the tone of her voice.

"Myles would have never sold them off as originals, Charlie. He didn't have it in him." Trust me, I would know, she added in her head.

"I agree, Jorja, but something doesn't add up. We've been through Myles' house, turned it upside down trying to find anything that might have caused him to be killed, and I can't recall seeing any paintings of Charing Cross Bridge at his house."

"Perhaps he stored them somewhere else? Maybe the bank?"

"I thought you said the pleasure was seeing them hang on your walls."

He was right. She had said that.

"What are you saying then, Charlie?"

"I'm not *saying* anything. It's just a theory, but what if that was the reason he got killed? What if Myles was robbed and the thieves thought you had the rest of the paintings at your gallery? They would need the full set, right? So, what if they broke into his house first to get the first ten, then finished the job breaking into the gallery for the remaining two. Perhaps you being there took them by surprise and Ewan drove by, saw the lights on, and got in the way of the robbery."

Oh, how she would love that to be the truth, she thought.

The car pulled up behind the ambulance at the hospital.

"I don't know, Charlie. All I care about right now is Ewan."

Charlie leaned over and opened the car door for her.

"You go ahead and stay with him. I'll check in with you in a bit. I think I'm onto something so I would like to run it past the chief inspector. From what I know of the man, he is most likely burning the midnight oil at the station."

She said goodbye and followed the paramedics into the hospital. Ewan's face was sallow and tubes ran from his arm into an IV bag a nurse snatched from the paramedic as soon as they rolled him through the doors. Within seconds, several doctors and nurses swarmed around him and pushed her out of their way as they wheeled him off.

"How's he doing? Is he okay?" she yelled at them but was ignored.

A friendly voice came up from behind and gently told Jorja that it was best she took a seat in the waiting area until the doctor came to talk with her. She had no choice but to comply and allowed the nurse she didn't recognize to usher her to a large open area to her right.

"There's a coffee machine over there, not the best but it does the trick, and a chapel down the hall to your right." She paused briefly then continued. "It might be a while before I have any news so feel free to spend some time in the chapel. I'll come find you when the doctor's ready."

She smiled affectionately then turned and darted back behind her station. The look in the effervescent nurse's eyes stayed with Jorja where she now stood staring through the glass of a tall window to a large terrarium. Filled with plants, a small fountain and a few large rocks that looked like a snake was going to crawl out of it at any moment, she caught a glimpse of her reflection in the windowpane. Her hands were still covered in blood, so was her powder-blue blouse. If Ewan died it would be her fault. Maybe the residents of St. Ives were right all those years ago when they assumed she was nothing but trouble. Maybe they'd seen straight through her. She had tried to create a new life for herself, thought that she could do it there, in St. Ives but no matter how far she tried to run, to hide from her past, it was clear it would always haunt her. Because that person from her past was who she really was and who she would always be.

Her thoughts were interrupted when the female nurse's gentle voice suddenly spoke behind her.

"I thought you could do with this. There's a bathroom down that way." She handed Jorja a white tee shirt with the hospital logo on.

"Sorry, it's all I had, leftovers from our recent charity Fun Run. The gift shop on the second floor should have something warmer for sale if you want to pop up and have a look. They open in a little while."

"Thank you, this shirt is perfect."

"You know, dearie, the chapel is nice and quiet this time of night. You might want to swing by on your way back, just saying." She squeezed Jorja's arm gently and scuttled back to her post.

The nurse's suggestion left her feeling annoyed. It seemed everyone she knew or met constantly felt the need to tell her to turn to God, as if he would even want her. Like they were so certain he was the answer to all that troubled her, someone who could magically fix all she had done wrong in her life. From what she had heard, he was a God who easily forgave, but what if she didn't want him to forgive her? What then? Why could they not just let her be? Let her wallow in her regrets, pay for it the way she should, the way she deserved.

Fueled by her troubled emotions she set off toward the restroom. As the water washed the blood away from her hands, she watched the dark red change to a soft shade of pink before it swirled its way down the drain, disappearing as if it had never been there. If only it was that easy, she thought.

Not being able to stand the sight of her reflection in the mirror in front of her, she turned her back to it and hastily switched shirts, eager to get out of there. When she was done, she tossed her blood-stained blouse into the rubbish bin on her way out and stormed off to get a coffee.

But, as she passed the small chapel, it was as if a magnet pulled her body toward it. Perhaps it was the rebel in her, wanting to prove that she was right, wanting to test God's forgiveness and if it would extend to her. She felt her freshly cleansed hand reach for the door handle, hubris firm in her heart as she entered and took a seat in one of the narrow wooden pews of the small hospital chapel.

CHAPTER TEN

The nurse wasn't lying when she said the chapel was quiet before sunrise—too quiet Jorja had to admit. But she soon realized that her discomfort was because the solitude forced her to face herself. So, she sat there, staring at the large white cross as if she was waiting for something to happen. Maybe a preacher would sneak in from behind a hidden door, or a choir would start singing, or perhaps she waited for God to strike her, punish her once and for all and get it over with so she could move on with her life. But nothing happened.

She leaned over to pick up one of the Bibles from a little cradle behind the pew in front of her. She flipped through the thin pages in search of Leviticus, then gave up when she couldn't find it and flipped back to the index in the front of the Bible. When she eventually found the page number that sent her to the third book, she paged to chapter nineteen then scanned down to verse eighteen. She read the words:

'Do not seek revenge or bear a grudge against one of your people, but love your neighbor as yourself. I am the LORD.'

She read it twice; it still didn't make any sense to her. Her eyes lingered on the cross again as she wondered why Ewan had told her to read this scripture. He'd also told her to leave her anger to God. None of it meant anything to her, so she slammed the Bible shut and put it back where she'd found it.

With the same hubris she'd come in with now slowly multiplying, she was just about ready to get up when she heard a man's voice from somewhere behind her. It startled her, more so because once again she'd dropped her guard and hadn't heard him come in.

"Well, you must be desperate to come in here this early," he said sounding smug and amused.

She ignored him and got up to leave.

"Sorry, the meds are making me grumpy," he immediately apologized, draping his masculine arms over the pew in front of him.

She sat back down, not sure why she was so relieved to have found a reason not to have to go yet.

"I'm usually in here alone this time of the day. Early bird catches the worm and all that. The doctors will be passing through here when they change shifts in a few hours—that's when God is at his busiest, I reckon." He smiled and Jorja couldn't help noticing how attractive he was. Roughly her age, tanned skin, dark hair, and the bluest of blue eyes one could ever imagine. He looked her up and down.

"So, what's your story? I'm usually good at guessing but I will admit, I cannot decide if you are a patient or a visitor. It's a bit early for visitors but then you don't look like you are sick either, hence my conundrum," he winked.

"My friend got hurt, I'm waiting to hear." She suddenly felt acutely conscious of how she looked and she tucked her hair behind her ear.

"So you've come to pray for him, that's nice."

"No, I didn't come here to pray, and what makes you think it's a man?"

"Because women like you aren't the single type," he flashed his handsome smile again.

"Well, I am single." *Why was she telling him this?*

"Great to know. So why are you here then if you're not praying?"

She didn't know, so she didn't answer.

"Ah, now I've got it. You're blaming yourself, aren't you? What did you do, huh?"

"What? No, nothing, it's none of your business." She still didn't move to get up, found herself not wanting to for some strange reason.

"So you do feel guilty. Told you I'm good at this. I bet

you're here looking for absolution. Except, you think you aren't worthy of God's forgiveness. That whatever you did will be too big a sin for the man upstairs to forgive you." He studied her face. "Yeah, there it is. You're wondering why God's let you get away with it, why he's not punishing you instead of your friend."

He smiled then moved to sit next to her in the pew.

She wondered how it was that this stranger knew what she hadn't even fully come to understand yet. As he slipped in next to her, she noticed for the first time that he was wearing a dressing gown. He caught her eyes glancing at the hospital bracelet on his wrist.

"Yep, I'm a patient in case you're wondering. Been here on and off for almost four years now. AIDS." He waited for her to react the way most people did when they found out. Except she didn't. He looked puzzled.

"You're not shocked, that's a first."

"Should I be?"

"Most people are, thinking I must be homosexual and such."

"Sorry."

"Don't be. I guess this was what it took to find my own absolution. It's what finally brought me to my knees."

He looked pensive as if recalling the past.

Her brows pulled into a slight frown but she waited for him to tell her more.

"You're not the only one who has something to be

ashamed of, you know. We all have regrets over the choices we make in life. I looked for absolution too, didn't think I was worthy of God's forgiveness either. My life was a mess before I eventually came face-to-face with God. Addiction is the devil's secret weapon of choice. Drugs, food, alcohol, sex, you name it. I lost a lot of friends along the way, most of them my fault."

He fell silent then turned to study her face again.

"But you don't strike me as an addict, so which is it, huh? I'm guessing fame or fortune, the only two left in the box."

Jorja didn't say anything and he turned to face the front of the chapel. They sat quietly staring at the white cross before he eventually spoke again.

"Here's what I do know about absolution. You're never going to get it until you forgive yourself first. Sometimes you make it easy for God to get you to that point of forgiveness, but judging from the pain in your eyes, I'm guessing you have been fighting it for a while. So here you are, in the dead of night, alone in a hospital chapel facing your demons while your friend is fighting for his life. Maybe you had something to do with him being here, maybe you didn't. But you are going to have to face your afflictions and stop trying to run away from whatever it is that's haunting you, before it destroys you and all those around you. Take it from me. No sin is too big for God to wash away and correct our paths, and for the record, he's not in the business of punishing people just so he gets his way. He's waiting for you to make the first move. In order to heal, you have to stop pretending it isn't there and face it head on. Sometimes the very thing that brought you here tonight is God's way of nudging you to face your demons. The more you run, the harder God has to fight to get your attention. I waited too long. Don't let staring death in the face be the last resort."

He got to his feet then glided toward the door.

"I'll leave you be. I think you need the chapel more than I do today."

And as suddenly as he had sneaked up on her, he disappeared.

SHE MUST HAVE sat there staring at the white cross for at least another thirty minutes, alone in the chapel, trying to digest what the stranger had told her; figure out how he knew what she was going through. Perhaps the man with the piercing blue eyes was dead on and that the time had come to stop hiding. If God was waiting for her to make the first move toward turning her life around once and for all, then that's what she would do. She would face her past, her fears, and her enemies head on. Perhaps if she found closure she could forgive herself. Perhaps God would then forgive her.

She found herself whispering her intentions to God and asking him to help her, even if she thought she wasn't worthy. And as she sat unknowingly praying, the friendly nurse barged through the chapel doors behind her.

"The doctor is ready to talk to you now, Ms. Rose. Come, I will take you to see him." She smiled and beckoned for Jorja to follow her.

CHAPTER ELEVEN

It felt like an eternity before Jorja found herself buzzed into the ICU and she followed the nurse to one of the rooms. Ewan lay in the only bed in the room. A thick tube ran from his mouth into a nearby machine. She couldn't help noticing how peaceful he looked. She recognized the doctor. He was a local St. Ives resident, one of her less regular clients with a passion for abstracts. Paying attention to his body language, she watched as he stood deep in thought at the foot of the bed making notes on a medical chart on a metal clipboard. When he spotted her, he quickly pressed it against his chest as if he needed to keep its contents a secret before his arms crossed over it. Extra security, she thought.

"Miss Rose, I understand you were the one who brought Detective Reid in."

His eyes told the friendly nurse to stay. It sent a bolt of

panic into the pit of Jorja's stomach.

"Quit the formality, Gerald. It's not like we've never met before. Is he okay?" Jorja said, ignoring the backhanded question, her voice steely and without expression.

The doctor's cheeks flushed with embarrassment as if he'd just been caught in a lie, then he answered, his voice less formal.

"For now, yes. His case is complicated but we think he's stabilized and out of immediate danger. We'll monitor him and know more over the next twenty-four hours."

"You *think* he's out of danger. What does that mean?" Jorja pushed, suddenly annoyed.

"As I said, *Miss Rose*, his case is a complicated one, it's simply—"

"You said that already. Complicated isn't an answer so break it down for me, *Doctor*. Is he going to make it?"

Two could play this game, she thought, and crossed her arms while holding his gaze. He frowned and let out a sigh, looking irritated with her, but she didn't care. The look in her eyes intensified, letting the good doctor know that she wasn't playing around. He succumbed.

"The bullet did a lot of damage and he lost a substantial amount of blood. It shattered his scapula and deflected, rupturing his subclavian artery. We managed to remove most of the bone fragments but there is a significant risk of hemorrhages and pseudo-aneurysm formation. I am afraid it becomes a waiting game. We will monitor him very closely but he will be under sedation to reduce the risk and it is highly possible he will need a second operation. There is just no way of knowing at this moment. It is best you go home and try to get some rest, Doctor's orders. We will call you if anything changes. I'm sure the police will be in touch with you very soon too."

Dr. Barker dropped the clipboard into the basket that hung from the foot of Ewan's bed, sending a message that he was done with the conversation as directly as anyone could. When he walked past her the look in his eyes became accusing, as if he thought her to be involved with something illegal. The town's gossip had undoubtedly reached his ears, which also explained why he'd kept the conversation so formal. He promptly turned and left the room, nodding to the nurse to escort Jorja out.

WHEN THE TAXI dropped Jorja off at home, her head was still spinning. How was it that suddenly everything was caving in around her? Everything had been just fine for years, decades. Why had it suddenly changed? Could the patient with the piercing blue eyes have been right? Was this God's way of nudging her into correcting what she had done wrong, finding closure instead of hiding from her deepest, darkest past?

Deep in thought, she cuddled Vincent then popped a bowl of fresh food in front of him. He reminded her of Charlie's theory the night before. If Charlie was onto something, Myles' murder could very well have had everything to do with her. For one, the art he bought through her was missing, and then there was the murder weapon.

She glanced back at the clock on her kitchen wall—it had just gone 7 a.m. Her hands fumbled for her cell phone in her purse—she had snatched it from her desk at the gallery without checking if her phone was still in it before she and Charlie left for the hospital. Relieved when she found it at the bottom of her bag, she dialed the police station.

"Hello, is Sergeant Chapwyn in, please?" She didn't recognize the receptionist's voice.

She transferred the call without hesitation and Charlie's voice came on in less than two rings.

"Jorja, I thought you'd never call. How's Ewan, any news?"

"Hi, Charlie, sorry, I didn't have news until a short while ago. He's not doing that well. The bullet shattered his clavicle and ruptured an artery. He's in ICU, under sedation. There is a chance it might lead to an aneurysm so they need to keep an eye on him. The doctor said his case was complicated and that there's nothing we can do but wait."

Charlie sighed heavily, his voice less enthusiastic when he spoke again.

"We're going to catch whoever did this, Jorja. I have every station from here to Bristol looking for this guy. Thanks to Ann's curiosity, her shop's security camera picked up an image of the man. Blurry, but at least it's something. A week ago, I mocked her for using it to spy on everyone, but low and behold, it finally served its purpose. Anyway, like I said, we're going to find this guy, Jorja."

"Thanks, Charlie. Any chance you could show me his picture. Maybe I can corroborate that it was the same guy."

"I thought you said you didn't really see the guy."

"I didn't, but maybe I'll remember something." She quickly corrected herself. She needed to see for herself if it was the same man who was outside her shop the day Myles died.

Charlie groaned telling her he was wrestling with the decision then he whispered, "I'm supposed to wait for clearance first, that's why I haven't been able to bring you in for questioning yet. Give me a day or so. I think since you were a victim too it's only fair to see if it might jar your memory or something. I will send it to your email once I get the thumbs-up. You can have a look and let me know if you recognize him. Sound good?"

"Sounds good, yes, and, Charlie, any weight behind that theory of yours? Do you still think they were after the Claude Monet collection?"

She bit her bottom lip as she waited for his answer.

"Yep, my chief inspector agrees. The paintings are nowhere to be found so it has become our primary motive. He's in talks with someone at Scotland Yard as we speak. I guess we will know more soon. We don't usually handle this type of thing here in St. Ives, you know. With Ewan in hospital, I'm a bit out of my depth here. But I do know they will most probably need you to hand over Myles' purchase receipts and all the paperwork related to the paintings, so hold onto those for now, please. And Jorja, perhaps don't leave town or anything. I know with the art fair coming up and all you probably need to pop up to London, but you might want to stay put. We don't want to draw any more suspicion to you."

He bit his tongue the moment the last sentence left his lips, but it was too late. Jorja had already realized what was going on behind the scenes.

"Of course," she responded without emotion.

WHEN THEY ENDED the call Jorja knew exactly what she needed to do. It didn't take much time for her to lock her doors and windows before she made her way up to the hidden space beneath the floor inside her bedroom cupboard. Her heart thumped as she retrieved the small leather duffle bag and tipped the contents out onto her bed. With nervous energy now pumping through her body, her fingers moved quickly over the contents on her bed, snatching up the radio pager when she found it. From the drawer in her bedside table, she found a new single cell battery and popped it into the pager. As she waited for the device to come alive she threw her head back, shut her eyes, and drew in a deep breath, exhaling slowly as her fingers moved between the buttons.

The device connected to the private radio signal almost

instantly and a fresh wave of nerves washed over her. She typed in the message.

'You said to get in touch if ever I was in trouble. Well, I'm in trouble.'

When she was done, she tossed the pager onto her bed as if it were hot and had just burned her hand, and then took a seat next to it to wait. She stared anxiously at the small LCD screen, it took longer than she remembered it taking back then, so she jumped up and nervously paced the bedroom. For a brief moment doubt dropped into her stomach. Perhaps the radio transmission was obsolete—it had been so long and no one used pagers anymore.

But a few moments later, the message notification blinked on the small screen. Her heart nearly stopped, causing her fingers to shake as she opened it to read.

Pick me a few sunflowers

The corners of her lips instantly lifted when she saw the single line of text flash across the screen. Some things never change, she thought fondly as she turned the pager off and dropped it back onto the bed. The alarm clock next to her bed flashed 7:42 a.m. If she left by eight she should be in London around two, leaving her an hour to get to their meeting place. It would be tight but she might just pull it off if the traffic played along. The meeting should be quick, a few hours at the most, so she could be back home before midnight, before anyone realized she had left town.

CHAPTER TWELVE

K nowing she had to take the long way out of St. Ives in order to remain undetected by the residents, or worse, the authorities, Jorja was well on her way in less than thirty minutes. She had managed to take a quick shower and got rid of the hospital tee shirt, replacing it with a plain white tee, a pair of dark-blue denim jeans, and the black leather jacket she hadn't worn in almost twenty years. Surprised it still fit she glanced at herself in the car's rear-view mirror. She had swept her hair back over her head, leaving it to curl slightly at the nape of her neck instead of it waving softly around her face, the same way she used to wear it when he last saw her. She was nervous, anxious even, more about seeing him again than being seen leaving town.

Her hands tensed around the steering wheel when she eventually reached the A30 bypass toward London. With her heart thumping hard in her chest, she now knew that there was no turning back. She'd known the moment she got into her car, always known that she'd only be able to run from her past for so long and that this day was bound to come. Yet, she had secretly hoped it never would.

When she reached the outskirts of London five hours later, she decided to leave her car at a small roadside hotel near Heathrow Airport—one she had used plenty of times in the past when she was on a job. She had thought it best to take the train into Trafalgar Square and go on foot from there. Partly to circumvent the traffic, but mostly to ensure she wasn't followed. She had been careful when she left town and hadn't seen anyone follow her to the city but then again she had been recently surprised one too many times by intruders she never saw coming. She was rusty and that was enough cause for her to be extra cautious— and extra anxious.

The hotel looked exactly as it had when she had last seen it, apart from it having a new name. She parked her car in the farthest corner under a large tree and out of sight of the surveillance cameras she had spotted as she approached; the second thing that had changed since she'd last been there. She took a moment to calm herself before grabbing her small satchel from the passenger seat. When she was certain no one was around, she reached inside and took out her SIG. She had loaded the clip at home before she left but she did one more check, then slipped it back in place. With the safety on, she tucked it inside a concealed pocket of her jacket, zipped up her bag, and swung it onto her back as she got out of the car.

Somewhere to her right, she spotted movement, but when she looked there was nothing there. She paused for a moment, just to be sure, but still didn't see anyone. Brushing it off as her mind playing tricks on her, she set off toward the train station a block away. She would reach Trafalgar Square via Paddington and Charing Cross stations and then it would be a quick walk to the National Gallery. Being back in the city excited her. She loved the tranquility of St. Ives but more often than not, she felt claustrophobic, trapped, and was reminded of where she had grown up. All she wanted to do from the moment she'd turned sixteen was run away, travel the world, see any town that would take more than fifteen minutes to walk across. A lot of good that did her, she thought, as she sat down on the train. After finally managing to escape a small town, life had forced her back. The very thing that once made her feel trapped now made her feel safe. Or did it?

THERE WERE ALREADY HALF a dozen passengers in the railcar plus three more who got on with her; a young couple, and a man she guessed to be in his late sixties. He sat a few seats down from her, took out his newspaper, and buried himself in its pages until they reached Paddington. Switching platforms she noticed he also switched and got onto the Charing Cross train with her, again seated a few seats away from her. Something inside her warned of danger and her body tensed. Her eyes fixed on his paper, watching closely to see if his eyes trailed the writing on the page as they would when one read from left to right. They didn't. Instead, they remained fixed in one spot on the middle of the page as if his attention was on his peripheral vision instead. She decided to put him to the test and got up to move to an opposite seat. As soon as she sat down, he turned the page and shifted his sights, practicing the same ritual. She homed in on the date of the newspaper. It was three days old, enough to tell her that her instincts were accurate. She was being followed and it was not by a six-foot-three man with broad shoulders.

Her heart pounded against her chest as they neared Charing Cross station. This was her only chance to lose him. There were about ten more passengers on the train, four of whom were a group of students huddled together near one of the exit doors.

Timing was everything.

As the train slowed into the station she readied herself, tensing her legs up to bolt for the door when the time came. In her experience, there was always a chance that he might be much younger—and less rusty—than his disguise portrayed, so she would have to be especially quick. Once the chime sounded she knew she had only three seconds at the most to exit before the door closed, less if the train was running late and needed to make up for lost time. Her eyes darted back to him. His body was rigid, tense, ready to move, his eyes pinned on the same spot in the paper. When the train stopped and a few passengers disembarked, she remained seated, all the while keeping an eye on the old man whose body language now seemed unsuspecting and more relaxed behind his paper. Her bluff had paid off. The chime sounded and she counted off the timing in her head. He looked up at her as if he sensed what she was planning.

Timed perfectly, Jorja was on her feet and charging for the door. He was as quick, right behind her. So close that she could smell his sweaty armpits. But she was quicker and slipped through just in time before the door fully shut between them. When she turned back, she found the man pressed against the door's window, his fingers wrestling to open the door. From beneath the bushy white eyebrows she now knew were not his own, his eyes were angry, warning her that she had not yet won.

FOLLOWING HER NARROW ESCAPE, Jorja picked up her pace until she reached her destination. She knew the National Gallery like the back of her hand. It had been the place she visited most often when she absconded from school. She would go to school in the morning for registration, then sneak away between classes to catch the nine thirty train to London. She would walk into the gallery by 1 p.m. like clockwork every Wednesday. Being back there again had her feeling giddy. As she took the stairs to the second level, she glanced at her wristwatch. She was early. It would give her time to compose herself, prepare. She lingered over the paintings on the way to Room 43. Corbet, Delacroix, Monet, all artists she adored. Excitement welled up inside her as she entered the Van Gogh room. Her eyes fell on the artist's *Sunflowers* painting and she took a seat on the empty bench in front of it. Painted in 1888 the oil on canvas painting lured her in as it had always done since the first day she laid eyes on it. She compared her life with the different stages of the sunflower's life cycle as was depicted in the painting. From young bud through maturity, and eventually, decay. She couldn't help wondering if she was in the maturity stage facing decay. But she shrugged it off as her poetic side running away with her and that she was still a long way from decay.

In the stillness of the empty exhibition room, she heard his footsteps approaching, sensed his presence in the room. But she couldn't bring herself to turn and look. She wasn't ready; it had been so long. Her heart skipped a beat, her hands felt clammy. Suddenly she felt her body temperature rise and was certain she was going to erupt at any moment.

Then his deep, warm voice came up behind her and instantly melted her insides.

CHAPTER THIRTEEN

"Well, aren't you a sight for sore eyes?"
He took a seat next to her, his body warm and safe and his presence as magnetic as she remembered. When their eyes met, she instantly knew why the stranger in the hospital chapel had felt so comforting. His piercing blue eyes and tanned skin had reminded her of him.

"Hello, Ben," she greeted him, her voice gentle and full of emotion.

Their eyes remained locked for what seemed like an eternity, allowing them to return to the last time they were together, to remember what they once shared.

When a small group of school kids and their teacher entered the room behind them, the commotion pulled them back into the present and Jorja spoke first.

"How have you been?"

A small smile broke across his face.

"You mean since you broke my heart and disappeared?"

"I had no choice, Ben."

"I know. You did what you had to and life went on." He scanned her face. "You look just the same, Georgina."

"So do you, Ben." She scanned the room then continued. "No one calls me that anymore though. It's Jorja now, Jorja Rose." She waited for his reaction.

"Jorja Rose. Suits you. That explains why I could never find you." His voice cracked and his body suddenly tensed up.

There was nothing she could say that would fix what was already done, so she allowed the silence to heal what was broken, and turned her gaze to the painting.

"This was our first," he broke the silence. "I remember it as if it were yesterday. We were just kids, but oh, that thrill."

"We were lucky. If it were not for Mr. Evans, we would have ended up in juvie. I still don't know why he covered for us."

"He liked you, almost as much as he liked this place. Besides, he was close to retirement. He probably saw it as a way to cash in on his retirement sooner, I reckon."

Ben turned to study her face.

"Do you miss it?"

Jorja tensed up. She knew the answer to that question all too well.

"I do, more than I should. But it's been twenty years and a lot has changed since then."

She found him looking down at her left hand.

"That has never changed."

It was her turn to look at his hand. A narrow white imprint where a ring had once been traced the tanned skin around his ring finger. It was as if someone had stabbed a hot poker through her heart.

"This was a mistake." She got up to leave, unable to fight the betrayal that threatened to make itself known in her eyes.

"Georgina... Jorja, wait! It's not what you think."

"I shouldn't have come, Ben, it's not fair to pull you back in. I'm sorry."

But as she headed for the door, she froze when her eyes found the man from the train entering the exhibition room. He had seen her too and started moving around the group of kids who stood huddled together around their teacher in the middle of the room.

"I'm guessing this is why you called me," Ben said quietly next to her.

She didn't need to answer. He could see it in her eyes as she turned to face him again.

Ben took both her hands in his. "He's not going to do anything in here, not with those kids around anyway."

"That might be, Ben, but there's only one way out of here and he's not going to just let us leave."

"What do you know of him?"

"Nothing, I spotted him on the train for the first time. But he isn't as old as he appears. That much I do know."

Ben's eyes revealed something familiar and she instantly knew what he was suggesting.

"You can't be serious, Ben."

"How sure are you that there is only one way out of here?"

He was teasing her with his handsome smile and the twinkle in his crystal blue eyes.

"It's been two decades, Ben. It won't work, not to mention that we aren't kids anymore."

Ben's smile widened.

"Do you see another way out of here? Besides, from where I'm standing, you're what, maybe five pounds heavier? We can totally do this."

She hated when he was right.

"Good. Now, I happen to know the trigger is still in exactly the same spot. One would think they would have upgraded the security system by now, but like a few other things, nothing has changed. So I guess today is our lucky day. Ready?"

"Ready."

She wasn't but it was irrelevant anyway. Her body simply couldn't resist. She craved the adrenaline like the desert craved the rain, and she couldn't stop it.

She glanced back at the old man who stood firm, guarding the exit door, his hand under his bomber jacket as if he held something in place.

Every fiber in her body was suddenly alive with excitement, just like it used to be when the two of them were on a job.

Her eyes found the floor tile roughly two feet to the left of the *Sunflowers* painting and she stepped on top of it. She heard the near-silent click and nodded to Ben that it had worked and that it was his turn. His hand reached to touch the spot on the wall to the right of the painting, then pushed down firm as they listened out for the second click. The sound came just as it had all those years ago. Excitement surged through their veins, their eyes fixed on each other in an almost trance-like state. Behind them the old man was moving in on his target, ready to finish what he had been instructed to do.

But Jorja and Ben were undeterred. She would have to be quick. Ben's eyes confirmed her thoughts. Jorja felt that familiar rush flood her body as she simultaneously lifted her feet and leaped onto the tile next to Ben. The alarm sounded loudly in the room and seconds later the wall swallowed both of them along with Van Gogh's painting, depositing them into the small safe room on the other side of the wall.

There was not another second to spare as their bodies squeezed up against the wall in the much too narrow chute. As if it were only yesterday, they were still perfectly in accord and she already had her foot atop his cradled hands that lifted her through the vent opening above their heads. Once inside the duct, she reached down to help Ben up from the chimney-like space. The air duct was smaller than it had seemed when they were young but they had done it. They crawled through the space, twenty yards further then turned down another vent until it opened up into a storage cupboard positioned on the other end of the historic building. She watched as Ben reached into his back pocket to retrieve two metal tools that he quickly used to unlock the door. It took three more minutes before they exited the back of the building and escaped through the service entrance into St. Martin Street. Behind them, they heard the police sirens rush toward the gallery as they disappeared into a shopping alley that led to Charing Cross station. Once they were underground and out of sight, they stopped for the first time while they waited for the next train.

Excitement surged through their bodies; their cheeks flushed and their bodies were on fire.

"I cannot believe we got away with it!" Jorja said, her smile so wide she did not think it was still possible.

"Twenty-odd years and they're still running the same safety triggers. Unbelievable," Ben echoed.

"Oh, no you didn't! You didn't know, did you? You guessed. Tell me you didn't, Ben!"

"It worked, didn't it?" He laughed, amused that she had caught him in his bluff.

"I can't believe you tricked me into thinking you knew it hadn't changed. What if they'd caught us, huh? What if they had changed the security?"

He pulled her into his arms, tucked an unruly lock of

hair behind her ear.

"I would've never let that happen, Georgina. We were born for this. You said it yourself. You miss it. Come on, I saw your face just now. You loved it. Just like the old days. We can do it again, Georgina, make up for the time we missed."

When his face came in to kiss her, she pushed herself away and turned her back on him before she turned to face him again.

"No, we can't, Ben. Too much has changed. I have a new life, a safe life, at least until recently. We have moved on. What we had back then was great, the best years of my life. But you have moved on too. You are married now, and that changes everything."

Ben shook his head with amusement.

"There it is again, the same flaw you've always had. What was the first thing I taught you, huh? Never. Assume. Anything."

Jorja's brow creased in a curious frown as she searched for how she had assumed wrongly.

"Was, Georgina, was. I was married, a long time ago. When you suddenly upped and left my heart was broken. I looked everywhere for you, gave up after eight years. I couldn't work anymore. My mind wasn't in it. So, I started to drink, heavily, hoping to drown my heartache. That's when I met my wife, in the local pub. She ran the bar, got me to an AA meeting. I have been sober ever since. Two years ago she died, caught in the crosshairs of a nasty pub brawl when she worked an event in South London. I never shed one single tear. And that's when it hit me. I was her husband; I should have mourned her, except I couldn't even bring myself to cry at the funeral. The hole I had in my heart was the one you had left behind, not her. It has always been you, Georgina. I have never gotten over you."

CHAPTER FOURTEEN

As Ben's words echoed in the hollow spaces of the underground train station, melting the invisible wall of ice Jorja had built up around her, another hollow sound exploded into the air and stopped in the concrete pillar inches away from them.

They flinched and ducked behind the column.

"You okay?" Ben asked.

"Yeah, you?"

Another bullet hit the concrete before he could answer. Ben popped his head around to find the shooter.

"There, on the train!" Jorja pointed to the train that had just pulled in on the opposite side of the train tracks.

"That wasn't where the first bullet came from," Ben said, still searching.

"And it isn't the old man from the gallery either. It's someone else," she added.

"I hate to tell you this, Georgina, but it looks like you might have a bounty on your head. I spot two more over there. Any idea who's trying to kill you?"

She didn't answer.

Another bullet came from somewhere behind them. People were screaming, crouching down behind trashcans and pillars. The sound of an approaching train and the sudden rush of warm air pushing toward them in the underground tunnel alerted them that a train was fast approaching and Jorja flashed a look at the information board above them. It shattered into a million pieces that rained down on top of them. Crouched behind the wooden bench, Jorja scanned the area for the multitude of shooters who were now opening fire on them from all directions. She spotted two men on the stairs taking aim to shoot.

"There are two more coming down the stairs! We need to get out of here!" she announced.

"I agree, we're sitting ducks."

"There, a train's coming!" Jorja said as another bullet flew through the air and brushed the sleeve of her jacket.

"Are you hit?" Ben yelled when she let out a moan.

"No, I think it just grazed me."

A police whistle rang repeatedly from the entrance of the subway, taking care of the two shooters on the stairwell who quickly scattered out of sight. The shooter in the train on the opposite side of the platform shot off one final bullet as his train pulled away, taking him with it. The bullet clanked hard against one of the metal bolts in the bench in front of Ben and Jorja, sending splinters up in a cloud above their heads.

"That leaves one more shooter according to my count," Jorja said once they had taken shelter behind the pillar again.

"He's not going to shoot, the place is already crawling with coppers. I say we hop on this train and see if we can get out of here."

The incoming train pulled into the platform; oblivious to the chaos it had just missed. But the conductor was already being informed, as was evident when he stopped to listen to the warning come in on his two-way radio before he promptly turned back and disappeared into the train to quickly shut the doors.

The pair didn't waste any time and they bolted for the train's doors, squeezing through a millisecond before the doors locked behind them. In their wake, the travelers on the platform were now in full panic where they had crouched down behind benches and billboards, many of them now crying in fear while half a dozen police officers searched for the gunmen amongst them.

"We need to blend in," Ben told Jorja when he spotted a few police constables approaching the stationary train.

They sat down on either side of two youths who were too busy on their electronic devices to notice the commotion. Moments later a door was flung open and a police officer stepped aboard. His eyes searched for any suspicious activity, glancing over Ben and Jorja who looked directly at him before he stepped off and moved toward the next coach.

Their ruse had worked.

When the train finally got the 'all clear' from the police it slowly pulled out of the station. But instead of feeling secure and out of danger, Jorja couldn't help but feel the exact opposite. On edge and watching their backs, they got off at the next stop and jumped into a taxi. There was one place they knew they would be safe, a place where no one would find them.

The taxi dropped them in a residential area in Kensington West where they watched it drive off before they crossed the street and walked in the opposite direction. Certain they weren't followed, they zigzagged between the shop-lined streets and soon reached their destination: a small corner shop with a faded sign above its door that read 'Dry Cleaners & Laundry.' The weathered bright blue wooden door was locked with a thick chain and marked with a yellowed paper in a plastic sleeve that was nailed onto the wood. The handmade signage announced that the shop was no longer in operation and had closed down.

They lingered in front of the store, scanning the immediate area for anyone who might be watching them, relieved when their surveillance turned up clear. As if one person they slipped out of sight into the short dead-end street that ran alongside the building. There was an old gunmetal gray Volvo station wagon parked to one side along with several large dumpsters behind it.

"You still have her?" Jorja asked, referring to the car.

"She might have a lot of mileage on her but she still purrs like a kitten."

"I think you fell in love with this car the moment you got behind the wheel, Ben Colebrook. Feels like yesterday," Jorja smiled as he pushed one of the dumpsters away. Behind it, a narrow steel staircase led to a basement entrance on the side of the laundry shop.

"I fell in love with a lot of things during that trip." He looked back and smiled before his thumb unlocked a small panel hidden behind a brick in the wall. He was quick to enter the security code followed by a retina scan before the tempered black steel door in front of them clicked open and invited them to quickly step inside.

The narrow passageway led them through a labyrinth of short passages below ground until it opened into a large space that was positioned directly below the laundry shop. When Ben turned the lights on and lit up their underground safe house, Jorja's face lit up along with it.

"It looks just the same, nothing's changed," she remarked as she wandered through the space, stopping at the workstation that was covered with high-end computers and other tech.

"You're still active. I thought you quit."

"I did, and no, I'm not still active. I just like to keep an eye on things, make sure I keep up with the times and such."

He reached into the nearby fridge and pulled out two Pepsis.

"Sorry, I don't keep any alcohol anymore."

"I don't drink much anyway, Pepsi's fine."

She took several sips and sat down on the leather sofa they had once acquired together from a local second-hand street vendor.

"Right, shall we get to work and find out who those guys are and why they're after you?" Ben prompted as he took a seat behind the computer station. "And while I'm at it, I might as well wipe the security footage of our little museum theatrical." He smiled as he set to work, then added, "Okay, tell me what you know."

"There isn't that much to tell really. I own a small art gallery—"

She stopped when he looked up at her with a wide grin.

"Of course you do. I don't know why I didn't think of tracking you down through the art galleries. I'd just assumed you wouldn't go near it after everything that went down." He stopped and laughed. "Now who's the one who broke my assumption rule? I guess you gained an advantage over me, huh? You knew I wouldn't check the art circles; it was too obvious. You always were the clever one."

Her eyes met his with a smile before she continued.

"One of my regular clients bought Monet's Charing Cross Bridge collection from me. I'd won it in a Muller's auction a year ago and agreed that he could buy it from me one piece a month. They weren't originals," she quickly added when Ben looked at her with intrigue.

"Anyway, there was this man, in the street opposite my shop, just staring at me through the window."

"What did he look like?"

"Very tall, I'd say at least six three, broad shoulders, and bald. Myles, my client, said something to him. I thought he just welcomed him to St. Ives like he usually did with visitors but the next thing I know Myles ends up murdered in my backyard, the murder weapon: a handmade copper rose, left neatly on his chest. The police seem to think he was murdered because of the paintings but I'm not so sure. Only a novice would mistake them for originals, and that rose, the significance is too blatant to ignore. I think it was intended to warn me."

Ben's fingers were moving over the keyboard faster than she could talk.

"Got it."

"What?"

"The case file. St. Ives, huh? Not the most secure little police station I'll have you know."

She smiled. "I'd forgotten how good you are."

"Shame on you, Georgina! There isn't much I can't find. Except of course you." He paused then continued running his fingers over the keys. "So, the paintings are nowhere to be found. No wonder they think that's what motivated the murder." He kept typing, then paused and looked at her with concern. "You left out the part where you were attacked in your shop. That changes things."

His attention went back to the computer.

"As for the murder weapon, you're right, Georgina. That's a unique piece of art." His fingers kept moving. "Well, now isn't that interesting?"

Jorja got up and leaned in over his shoulder. An entire collection of long-stemmed copper roses had popped up on his screen. As Jorja skimmed the caption beneath the photo, her heart practically stopped beating.

She turned and paced up and down the space behind him.

"I knew it! I was right. He's found me, Ben!"

CHAPTER FIFTEEN

G ustav Züber smoothed back his silver hair with his palm, following each stroke with his tortoiseshell comb until every strand of his hair was perfectly in place. It was what he did whenever his anger got the better of him, a calming ritual of sorts. His thumb and index finger closed over the silver thumb notch on the vintage comb, which he then carefully placed back into its pewter case. Admiring the raised relief design on the comb case he took his time treasuring the moment before he neatly slipped it back inside the pocket of his suit's jacket. It was moments like these he made sure to savor after he got released from prison several years back. He was a man of impeccable taste and enjoyed the luxuries of life, even more now that he was able to enjoy them again.

His arthritic hands tidied the knot of his yellow silk tie as he took one final glance in the antique mirror before he turned to face his henchman. From beneath his bushy gray eyebrows, his near-black eyes were angry, a sign to his subordinate of what was to come. When he spoke his tone was steely, another sign that he was fighting hard to contain his anger.

"I was told you had experience, Ludwig. That your methods are far superior to those of your counterparts. So I find myself, how shall I say this, perplexed." He repositioned the Fabergé cufflinks that had once belonged to Edward VII before he spoke again. "I mean it's not like she is some super ninja with supernatural powers. She's a woman, nothing more. And by now, probably several pounds heavier, out of shape, and baking scones in an untidy kitchen with a couple of brats running around her. How hard could it have been, huh?"

"She had help, Herr Züber, a man."

Gustav's eyes narrowed.

"A man, one man. Tell me, Ludwig, how many men did you send after her?"

"My entire task team, six men in total."

"Six men. Against one woman, and a man. I don't know if I should laugh or cry. Does this not sound ridiculous to you? I mean, you had one job to do, Ludwig, and you failed, miserably. Tell me now, did I make a mistake hiring you?"

The man facing him squared his shoulders, pushed out his chin, and answered in a firm voice.

"I will get the job done, Herr Züber. She won't get away this time."

Gustav stepped three paces forward to close the gap between them, clasped his hands behind his back, and pushed his pointy jaw mere inches away from Ludwig's face.

"Good answer, because if you fail this time I will personally make sure you don't see another sunrise. My time in prison might have aged me but it has also taught me a few new skills that even an old man like me can utilize with ease. It has taken me years to track her down, years, and I will risk everything to finally give her what she deserves. Do not mess it up. Now get out of my face before I regret giving you another chance."

His hired hand did not hesitate and promptly spun on his heels and left.

JORJA WAS STILL PACING the floor, her body tense and her emotions running wild. Driven by fear and uncertainty she moved across the floor like a deer trapped between hunters.

"I should have known it was just a matter of time before he'd find me. How he did, I would not know. *You* couldn't even find me. But that rose, I was right. It *was* intended to scare me. Artem Sokolov is not a man to mess with. I was convinced he was KGB then and I'm even more convinced of it now."

"Okay, you need to get a hold of yourself, Georgina. There is no evidence he is behind any of this."

"You're joking, right, Ben? How do you not see it? It's right there, on your computer screen, a whole bunch of roses just like the one used to kill Myles. We need to send it to Ewan," she caught her breath as she spoke the words, then hurried to her bag on the couch in search of her phone. She had forgotten to check in on him.

"Who's Ewan? Ah, not to worry, his name was in the police report. He's the detective inspector on the case, the one who got shot by the guy who attacked you in your gallery."

She nodded as her eyes scanned over the messages and five missed call notifications on her phone.

Her fingers hastily glided across her phone's screen before she placed it firmly against her ear.

"Charlie, it's me, Jorja."

"Jorja, where are you? I've been looking everywhere for you."

"Yes, sorry, I got your messages, I was just... why, what happened?"

She bit her lip and sent up a prayer not knowing if God would even listen.

"It's Ewan, he's had to go back in for a second surgery. Something about bone fragments that got into one of his veins. It's not looking too good, Jorja."

He paused, then continued.

"Where are you, anyway? I went looking for you at your house but you didn't answer the door."

"I just needed to get some fresh air, Charlie, sorry. I will be home soon. Is he going to be okay?"

"They don't know. All we can do is pray for him and let God do the rest."

She ended the call, her heart encumbered with a mixture of guilt and anger.

Ben's eyes traced the lines of her face.

"How ignorant of me? Here I was, spilling my guts over my dead wife, declaring my undying love to you, and all the while you have a bloke back home."

"It's not like that, Ben."

"No? Seems like it to me. New name, new life, new love. I get it, it's blatantly obvious."

"No, it's not, Ben! Ewan is just a friend. A very dear friend who is fighting for his life in the hospital as we speak, and it's entirely my fault. Everywhere I go people get hurt. My parents, you, Myles, and now Ewan. It has been a lifetime of guilt over what I did to you. But I didn't have a choice. It's like I attract death or something. It doesn't matter what I do or how far I run, it always catches up with me. That's why I left! I had to, so you wouldn't get hurt."

She snatched her bag up and threw it over her back.

"I've got to go. I'm sorry, it was a mistake coming here."

Ben was quick on his feet to catch her by the arm.

"Don't go, not like this, okay? I'm sorry. I broke my

number one rule yet again. And you are wrong by the way; you are an angel but not an angel of death. I'm here for you, Georgina, Jorja, whoever you want to be. I will always be here for you, no matter what."

His ice-blue eyes had turned the warm, inviting turquoise color of an ocean paradise that instantly set her soul at ease. He was the only man she had ever loved, that would never change. Their souls were bound together no matter how much she tried to fight it.

Her mind flooded with the prophetic words the unknown patient in the chapel had imparted. It could not have been truer. She had to face her past; it was the only way.

"I can't stay, Ben," she whispered. "I have to finish this. I have been in hiding for twenty years and I cannot run anymore. If I run, I am nothing but a coward, a fraud."

His strong hands cupped her face.

"I couldn't agree more, but if you think I am going to let you go about it alone you're making a mistake."

"No, Ben, I can't risk it. You almost got killed earlier. Sokolov wants me, not you. I guess he has his score to settle after what I did to him. If I can find a way to pay him back the money, hopefully, he will back off, before someone else gets hurt."

"Georgina, it's not that easy, and you know it. He *has* money. The man is filthy rich and quite possibly involved with the KGB. You said it yourself. Artem Sokolov wants vengeance, and he won't stop until he gets it."

Jorja couldn't deny it. Everything Ben said made perfect sense. She couldn't do it on her own. Artem was a powerful man and she'd betrayed his trust, destroyed his reputation in the most embarrassing way possible. To meet his wrath on her own was insane, suicidal. She needed Ben now more than ever.

As if Ben knew she was still not convinced, he added,

"I can be of value to you, Georgina, help you, protect you, you know that. We've done it before and we can do it again, even after twenty years. We were a team once and we can be it again. It's like riding a bicycle," he winked, then almost instantly his face turned serious. "Besides, I don't think you have all the facts straight. Something doesn't quite add up."

CHAPTER SIXTEEN

J orja's insides did a summersault before it morphed into a heavy ball of knots in the very pit of her stomach. Fear rippled through her body as the weight of Ben's words warned her to brace herself.

"What are you saying, Ben?" Her voice was burdened with angst.

His hands cupped her shoulders and he pinned his eyes to hers.

"It's going to be okay, Georgina, trust me. Isn't this why you called me? Take a deep breath and come have a look at this."

He was right. She'd known Ben would get to who was behind Myles' murder long before law enforcement could. So, she let him steer her toward a chair next to his at the computer station then watched as he frantically started moving his computer mouse all over the screen, dupli-cating the same vigor with his fingers on the keyboard.

"What am I looking at?" she asked lacking patience.

"Almost got it, wait for it... there."

Several black and white photos popped up in layers on one of the other monitors. When the sequence ran its course, Ben's voice suddenly filled with excitement, as if he had already figured it out.

The first image was a shot taken by a surveillance camera pointed at her gallery's doors.

"That's my shop, how did you—?"

"Ask no questions, hear no lies, Georgie Porgie," he smiled with affection.

The name was what he used to tease her with and the fond reminder instantly released some of the tension in her shoulders. His computer mouse dragged the picture to one side, revealing another image taken with the same surveillance camera.

"That's the guy who stood watching you the day of Myles Brentwood's unfortunate demise, correct?" He zoomed in on the picture to display the man up close.

"It is, yes."

"And this guy here," he clicked then pointed to another photo, "is the guy who attacked you and your friend in your gallery the other night."

Again, he zoomed in.

"It's not the same guy," Jorja remarked.

"Exactly! Now, look at these photos over here. These

are the people who attacked us at the train station today. Look closely. Can you see the scar over this guy's face over here, above his left eye?"

She nodded as he pointed at one of the shooters then clicked and dragged another photo next to it on the screen.

"The guy who attacked you in your gallery is the same guy who shot at us today. See the scar? It's the same. But the man who stood watching you from outside your gallery doesn't have any scars, also, that guy is nowhere to be found on any of the train station or National Gallery's surveillance footage."

Jorja had leaned forward in her seat, quietly taking in all Ben had to show her.

"But wait, there's more!" he teased. "Look at the man outside your shop; you have a silk shirt, cashmere coat, powerful shoulders. Now compare it to the amateurs from the train station, even the man with the scar. Totally opposite, right? This guy outside your shop, he reeks of money, all the way from his shiny bald head down to his matte snakeskin shoes. While in direct contrast, the bunch from today looked more like a group of cheap bounty hunters. You have denim jackets, ripped jeans, and scruffy, cheap shoes that look like they just stepped off a building site. Trust me, I know a bounty hunter when I see one, and these, my dear, were probably picked up in a backstreet pub somewhere. I can smell them from a mile away."

He played one of the surveillance videos, then added.

"Notice how disjointed their shooting is. There's no

plan, no thought for execution. Like they had each received a random text message with your photo and the instruction to hunt you down, no plan, no sequencing, nothing."

He waited for the penny to drop.

"They're not connected."

Jorja's voice was low and without cadence, her face suddenly pale.

"We're dealing with two unrelated enemies here, Georgina, and I think we both know exactly who they are."

She slumped back in the chair, staring at the images on display in front of her. In that moment, her worst fears had suddenly come true. Fear had gripped her by her throat and sent uncontrollable tremors to her hands. Barely able to breathe she stared at the screen. Tears welled up in her eyes and spilled down her cheeks.

"I am as good as dead, Ben."

"Stop! Don't even think that," he said in a stern voice, jerking her from her woeful state.

She jumped to her feet and started pacing the floor, suddenly flooded with panic.

"How can you be so naive, Ben? It was bad enough knowing that I am up against Artem Sokolov and his entire Russian mob, but facing Gustav Züber simultaneously, I am completely outnumbered. I might as well write my obituary."

"Oh, there's the spirit. Give up without a fight. Boy, you were not kidding, were you? St. Ives has changed you all right. Where's the Georgina I knew, huh? The one who stood her ground and never backed down, for anything or anyone? The one who faced fear head on? Have you gone all soft on me in that salty Cornish air?"

He got up and went to fetch another soda from the fridge.

"I don't know what you're expecting of me, Ben. We aren't careless twenty-somethings anymore. I am almost fifty for crying out loud. Twice now I have been surprised by attackers, I never saw either of them coming and am clearly off my game—twenty years off my game."

Once more, she reached for her bag.

"I've got to go. Like I said, the further you stay away from me, the better. Thanks for your help."

She walked toward the exit.

"So you're going to do it again, are you, Georgina? You're going to walk out on me just like that, excluding me and making decisions *for* me instead of with me."

"I'm not making any decisions for you, Ben, I'm simply making sure you stay alive."

"Just like you did that day twenty years ago, right? And look how that's turned out."

"I don't know what you want from me, Ben. What would you have me do, huh? I never intended for that deal to go bad, but it did, and now I'm the one who's going to pay the price for it. Gustav Züber was the one who got greedy, not me. I was the one caught in the middle remember? He was careless, got caught, and almost dragged me down with him. If I hadn't blown the whistle on Züber's operation and disappeared, I *would* have gone down with him. I couldn't tell you what was going on even though I desperately wanted to. I protected you, Ben. Neither of them ever knew about you, and I would like to keep it that way. That's what allowed you to live a normal life for the past twenty years."

She turned to walk away then looked back at Ben. Tears had filled her eyes anew and seeing the sadness in his eyes broke her heart into a million pieces, just like it had all those years ago.

"Goodbye Ben."

"Don't do this, Georgina, please!"

But she had made her decision and ran out of the building as fast as her legs would carry her, knowing that if she looked back, she might not be brave enough to walk away a second time from the only man she'd ever truly loved. So she kept running, zigzagging through the streets until she found the underground entrance to the tube. When she finally got onto the first train heading toward Heathrow Airport, she could no longer control her tears and they flowed freely down her flushed cheeks.

Squeezed into a corner seat in the back of the train, her reflection stared back at her from the tiny window next to her. The woman in the glass didn't look like her at all. Every cell in her body felt weak, drained of life, and without hope. She thought of Ewan fighting for his life in hospital and the words spoken by the unknown patient in the chapel. She thought of Ben, of how things once were and how she would have done anything to have that again.

But then, as easily as her heart had filled with pain and despair, she was suddenly overwhelmed with anger. She had seen Gustav Züber's face flash before her, remembered what he'd done all those years ago and how he was to blame for all of this. The more she pondered on it, the deeper her anger festered.

By the time she found her way back to her car in the roadside hotel's parking lot, her anger had already turned to hatred. When she slipped in behind the wheel of her car, the woman who stared back at her in the mirror was no longer saddened or defeated. Instead, her eyes were darker, determined, and unaffected by any emotion.

She swiped away the smudged, black make-up that had settled beneath her eyes with the back of her hand, then smoothed her hair back in place. Her eyes fixed on the satchel that lay on the passenger seat next to her.

She had everything she needed right there with her. It was time she took matters into her own hands.

CHAPTER SEVENTEEN

Night had fallen by the time Jorja reached the once familiar address in South London. Though she had not been there in a very long time, not much had changed and she found the block of flats with ease. The small residential suburb was known to be one of the most dangerous boroughs in London and not safe for any woman to be in at night, much less alone. As she pulled up into a well-lit street nearby, she took out her gun and placed it in her pants' waistband underneath her tee shirt, then tucked her satchel out of sight underneath the driver's seat. When she got out of her car, she paused and looked out onto a courtyard surrounded by several three-story apartment blocks. The lights on the four edges of the courtyard were almost entirely broken and dim lights flickered on and off, casting long shadows from the buildings across the yard. At first glance, the neighborhood seemed quiet with not a soul in sight. But as she remembered all too well, her arrival would soon lure the residents out from their shadowy lairs like cockroaches to food. It took all of a minute for the first gang of rough youths to show themselves and she watched with caution as more soon emerged. From the dark shadows behind the isolated bleachers, a pit bull held firmly in place by a chain next to his master's leg, barked ferociously, ready to charge. She walked toward it, instantly recognizing the man she'd come there to see. He looked older, of course, but he wasn't the type to easily blend into any crowd. The dreadlocks that dropped down to just below his shoulders were now streaked with gray and even in the dark, she could see he still had more gold teeth than white ones. It was the feature that had awarded him the title of the most feared man in the neighborhood, and his name.

As on-trend with his fashion as always, the Jamaican man released a little bit of the chain, allowing his dog to charge several yards toward her before it got yanked back by the collar around his neck.

Surrounded by the bright orange glow of cigarettes in the dark, she kept walking slowly but steadily toward him, then stopped under the flickering illumination of a broken floodlight in the center of the courtyard.

The sharp sound of switchblades formed a choir all around her, accompanied by the incessant barking of the fierce dog mere feet from her. She looked straight at its owner, then announced herself.

"Andre, it's me, Georgina."

She heard the trigger of a gun being pulled back from somewhere to her right but remained firm in her stance.

Once again, the pit bull was allowed another few inches toward her. She knelt down and leaned toward the dog.

"Hey, there, old boy."

With exposed canines, the dog paused for just a second before his growling instantly turned to a friendly whimper while his tailbone dropped and sent his tail excitedly wagging. She leaned in closer, holding the back of her hand out for the dog to smell and lick.

"There's a boy. You like that. Don't you? Yes, you're not as fierce as you look now are you?" She smiled as the dog took pleasure in the tickling under his chin.

The chain released all the way and the dog leaped on top of her, nearly pushing her to the ground.

A deep gravelly voice came from the other end of the chain.

"It really is you, ain't it? Must be, because there ain't no one I've ever known that could hypnotize a pit bull like you. Your mojo has messed up every dog I've ever had."

Andre 'Mad Dog' Williams moved to join his dog, holding up the flat of his hand to his gang members to stand down.

"Venom, sit!" he ordered his dog.

Jorja pushed the excited dog off her knees and straightened up.

"Hey, Andre, it's been a while. It's nice to see you."

The mouth of the short beefy man in his early fifties opened wide to expose his gold teeth that glistened under the once working lights.

"You do know you have a half mil bounty on your head, don't you?"

"Only half a million? That's quite the insult." She smiled.

"Either way we might want to get you out of here. My guys are fine but I cannot say the same of Ludwig's bunch. Word on the street is he's hell-bent on finding you. Since he moved in here five years ago he acts like he's some kind of roadman or something."

He let out a shrill whistle to which the dog instantly reacted before he gave Jorja a firm hug.

"It's good to see you. Come; let's get out of here. I don't want no trouble tonight."

He snapped his fingers and five of his men formed a circle around them, shielding the pair as they walked into the nearby building. Once inside, two of the men stayed at the entrance, while the other three accompanied them into the flat.

"You did some decorating, I see." She smiled as she sat down on the leopard print sofa and allowed her eyes to take in the bright blue LED lights that trimmed the edges of the walls.

He handed her a beer then took a seat on a white fur-trimmed armchair opposite her. The smell of cannabis lay thick in the air.

"I thought you were dead, Gigi," he said, calling her by the nickname he had for her.

She didn't answer and he leaned forward, balancing his elbows on his knees while he lifted the beer bottle with his thumb and index finger in an almost upside-down manner to his mouth. When he'd had another quick sip, he put the bottle down on the floor between the brand-new pair of trendy Jordans on his feet.

"I'm guessing you soon will be though, huh, that's why you're here."

"I was hoping you would help me, yes."

"You know I will do anything for you, Gigi. We go back a long way. Dang, woman, you were my first customer, the one who put me on the map. I owe all this to you, my friend." He scooped to pick up his beer and took another swig. "So tell me, what do you need help with? I've got new guns, copper uniforms, transit vans, keys, what do you need, my old friend, name it."

"I need a new identity, a passport. I need to get into Switzerland."

His eyes narrowed.

"Don't ask, Andre, please. The less you know the better. How soon can you have it ready?"

"You know, Gigi, it doesn't take a genius to figure out

what you're planning. I just told you that Ludwig is all over this thing and that you have a bounty on your head. He might have gotten his name from that Beethoven guy whose music he's always humming, but he ain't no joke. His methods are brutal and from what I've heard, the Swiss man who hired him isn't messing around either. He is after your blood with vengeance. Now you're telling me you need to get into Switzerland. You've lost your mind, my friend."

Jorja crossed her legs and rested her beer on top of her leg.

"I don't have much of a choice, Andre."

"Gigi, you burned the man. Word on the street is he's been looking for you since he got out of jail. He'll never let you live."

"Well, he'll have to fight to get to me first. He's not the only one after me."

Her revelation had Andre wriggle uncomfortably in his seat.

"Tell me it's not who I think it is."

Her silence confirmed his suspicions and he was on his feet nervously pacing the space between them. He leaned in and spoke to her in a hushed tone.

"You've lost your mind going after these guys, Gigi! A burned convict is one thing, but KGB? That ain't no joke, fam!" he said, using the slang word for a close friend.

His dreadlocks bounced from side to side as he nervously shook his head.

"These guys are dangerous, Gigi. They'll kill you."

"Not if I get to them first."

"Then what, huh? You going to have a cup of tea with them over a friendly chat? That's crazy thinking, woman."

"I'm not the one who messed up, Andre. Gustav brought this on himself. He got what he deserved. He used me."

"Yes, and you ratted him out and the man spent fifteen years behind bars for it. Fifteen years is a long time to fester over what you did to him. That's a whole lot of hate and revenge bottling up inside a man."

"I did what I had to do to keep everyone safe. I wasn't going to let him take us down with him. Look, I'm not planning to kill the man, just get him off my back. I put him behind bars once before, maybe I can do it again. He's bound to have continued his illegal activities when he got out of jail."

"And what about the Russian guy, huh? He's the one you really should be worried about."

"I'm not sure yet. Maybe I can get back what he lost. That's worth far more to him than taking revenge on me. You aren't going to talk me out of it, Andre. I've hidden from these guys for twenty years and it stops here, right now."

The trendy gangster shuffled back into his chair and tilted his wild head to one side.

"From that speech, I'm assuming Ben tried to talk you out of it already."

"He doesn't know anything and I prefer to keep it that way."

"You're going after these guys on your own? Now I know you've lost your mind, woman."

"It's better this way, for everyone's sake."

CHAPTER EIGHTEEN

Andre was on his feet again, swinging his bottle of beer around like a mad man.

"You're insane, Gigi. The man's offered five hundred thousand quid for your head on a stick and you think it's going to be this easy. Sorry, Gigi, I cannot let you do it. It's suicide."

Jorja was on her feet now too.

"So you're not going to help me with the passport. Fine, I will just have to go to Nicolescu then. I'm sure he'll be just too thrilled to hear his arch-nemesis didn't have the guts to accept this job."

She turned to leave and heard Andre clicking his tongue in irritation behind her.

"You are still as bullheaded as ever, Georgina."

He'd only ever called her by her full name once, long ago when they first met.

"Fine, I'll help you, but on one condition."

She turned to face him.

"Name it."

"You take one of my men with you."

"Not going to happen, Andre. I have to do this on my own."

"Take it or leave it, Gigi. I can have the passport ready for you in fifteen minutes, and I'll do it at no charge, but you take Zeus with you, or I won't do it. I'm the best in the business and you know it."

She followed his eyes that indicated one of his men who stood to one side talking on a cell phone.

"That guy! He'll stick out like a sore thumb in Switzerland."

"I trust him and it's the only way I know you'll be safe. I'll have him tone down on the Jamaican flavor, but it's not negotiable."

She hesitated but knew Andre well enough to know he was only trying to look out for her.

"Fine, but he does it my way. What I say, when I say it, and how I say it. Deal?"

Andre was quick to respond.

"You need to fix your make-up before I can take a photo. Angie's got some make-up that should do the trick." He was referring to his latest fling who had been sitting quietly at the back of the room staring at her phone's screen.

They exchanged a brief smile and Andre came in to give her another hug.

"Thank you, Andre. I can't do this without your help."

"Just promise me you'll be careful, okay? You still owe me that bottle of Moët remember? I never did get it so this time I'm not having you disappear without getting what you owe me. Now get your face sorted out and let's get you on the first plane out of here."

ANDRE 'MAD DOG' Williams was just about finished with Jorja's forged travel document when a loud banging on the flat's door jerked them all to attention. Zeus was at the door first, gun in hand.

"Yo?" He shouted the slang greeting through the door but no one answered.

Andre's body tensed up and he nervously rushed the last bit of work on the passport. As if rehearsed a thousand times before, Angie was quick to hide away any evidence of her boyfriend's illegal activity in a small safe behind an obviously fake painting of the Mona Lisa, while the rest of Andre's protectors took up positions in each corner of the room.

Jorja's hand was on her gun now too where she had hidden in the nearby bathroom, leaving the door slightly ajar to keep an eye on events.

"Yo, speak up!" Zeus invited an answer again.

When no answer came back, he looked over his

shoulder for instruction from Andre who had just completed the passport and was already at the bathroom door where he handed it to Jorja.

"Stay here and let me handle this, okay?" he whispered to her and moved toward the flat's entrance.

His hand was on the gun that was tucked inside the waistband of his pants underneath his shirt while he readied himself and nodded for Zeus to open the door.

Five men followed by Ludwig burst through the door the moment he unlocked it and a maelstrom of switchblades and guns came at the unsuspecting party of Jamaican gangsters, pinning them against the walls before they had a moment to fight back. Angie screamed and ran to the bedroom, slamming then locking the door behind her. Close on her heels one of the rival gangmen was after her, passing the bathroom where Jorja had already locked herself inside.

Venom, the pit bull, barked ferociously before lunging at Ludwig's shins and sinking his teeth into his legs. His attack was countered by an angry fist against the side of his head that sent the poor dog yelping across the floor.

"Where is she, Mad Dog? I know she's here!" Ludwig shouted as he charged toward Andre and pointed his gun firmly against Andre's forehead.

"You just missed her, you fool, now get out!"

But Ludwig wasn't convinced and, with his gun still aimed at Andre's head, scanned the room.

"You're lying. She's mine, Mad Dog, do you hear me?

That money is mine! Now give her up before I make you regret it!"

"What money?" Andre bluffed.

The insult got him a backhand across the face after which his cautionary gaze met his opponent's angry scrutiny.

"You might think you have me with that gun pointed at my head, but this is my hood, bruv. Get out before I kill you with my bare hands." Andre's words were slow, controlled, and heavy with threat, emphasized by his sarcastic cant address for the term they used when referencing a brother by blood or friendship.

His threat invited a scoff from Ludwig. One the guy soon came to regret when, in one quick move, Andre seized his gun and turned the barrel full into his rival's face.

The skilled action took Ludwig by surprise and he retreated two steps. With the gun now in Andre's hands, aimed firmly at Ludwig's face, he drove his rival back toward the exit.

"Tell your men to stand down."

Ludwig hesitated.

"Don't make me ask you again, Ludwig. I ain't gonna be so nice second time round, bruv. There's a reason why I am still running things around here and deadbeat wannabes like you end up bleeding out on my floor."

With Ludwig's eyes fixed on the barrel of his gun, he

gave the command to his men who instantly backed away from Mad Dog's gang.

"Good, now get out of my house and never, ever point a gun at me or my friends again. Got it?" His lips pulled back like a rabid dog's, growling while he exposed his mouthful of gold teeth that threatened to rip out Ludwig's throat.

The action that drove home Andre's gang name had the intended effect and Ludwig turned and left, his men close behind him.

In the distance, police sirens pierced the night air, letting them know someone must have called the police about the disturbance. Angie slowly emerged from the bedroom, as did Jorja who came to stand next to Andre, her tone amused when she spoke.

"I see you're still scaring people off with that ridiculous fake rumor you invented. As if you could ever rip someone's throat open with those blunt teeth. You're as meek as that little puppy of yours, my friend."

"Yeah, well, don't go advertising that, Gigi. That rumor's what's keeping the scepter in my hand."

His attention turned to the sirens that grew louder by the second.

"We've got to get you out of here before the cops find you." He beckoned Zeus to join them. "My man Zeus will take care of you and, Gigi, it's not too late to back off."

She reached out and placed one hand on his shoulder.

"I need to do this, Andre. I'm tired of hiding. I'll see you again soon, my dear friend. Thanks for your help."

Her smile was warm and loving when she turned and left with Zeus on her heels, leaving the tough Jamaican exterior of her friend to nearly melt in a colorful puddle on the floor.

"You've got that right, and don't forget the Moët next time!" Andre yelled after her as he watched them escape into the chilly night air.

CHAPTER NINETEEN

Outside there wasn't a living soul in sight anywhere as the commune of hoodlums had scattered to take shelter in their homes as if nothing had happened. As Jorja and Zeus ran across the empty communal courtyard, bright blue lights flashed in the night sky as the police approached from the right.

"This way!" Zeus announced as he steered them down a footpath that ran between two blocks of flats away from them.

Tall overgrown shrubs lined the dark, narrow footpath and rustled noisily as they brushed past the thorny branches. The path wound its way between the properties until it opened to a large patch of grass circled by tall trees. She followed Zeus as he ran across the grass before he disappeared between two large horse chestnut trees.

"Come on, keep up before them coppers' cameras pick us up!" he yelled back when Jorja trailed too far behind.

A few yards further on they reached another footpath and their feet echoed loudly through the quiet night air.

"Where are we going?" she yelled at Zeus, who was already several yards ahead of her again.

He didn't answer.

She watched as once more, he disappeared over a slight mound and down the other side into the dark shadows between rows of thick bushes that led down to some woodland. When she reached the spot where he'd vanished between the bushes, he was nowhere to be seen. Stopping for a brief moment, she whisper-shouted his name into the darkness.

But he didn't answer.

She listened in the stillness of the night for sounds of his feet hitting the leafy bed or the conkers that lay strewn across the ground.

To her right, she heard a twig snap and instantly turned to look. Then suddenly leaves rustled behind her. She spun around to find Zeus's dark face right on top of her before his big strong hand closed over her mouth. She tried to scream but his hand was firm against her lips, muffling any sound that tried to escape from her mouth.

"Shut up!" he whispered from behind her ear while he pinned her back against his bulky body that seemed to devour her petite frame.

The damp leaves beneath her feet gave way and made

her slip in a futile attempt to fend him off. She pushed her body back against his as much as her weight would allow and, at first, she nearly managed to push him off balance. But he came back stronger.

"Give it up, woman! A million quid is too much dosh to say no to. You're not going to get away from me so quit fighting it! I ain't giving up."

But Jorja wriggled and fought back hard until she was close enough to a tree directly in front of her. Using his body as support, she walked her feet up against the tree's thick trunk and kicked herself back against Zeus's torso. The momentum had him fall flat on his back, inadvertently freeing her in the process. She was up on her feet in a flash and just as quickly had her gun in his face while she held him down on the ground with one foot atop his thick neck.

When his hands came up toward her legs to pull her off him, she firmed her grip around her weapon and aimed the barrel at the frown lines between his eyes.

"Don't even think of it, Zeus."

Jorja pinned her focus on Zeus's face where she still had him immobilized on the ground under her foot. Behind his small eyes, something hinted at him being nervous, almost scared, and she knew it wasn't because of her. She watched his eyes darting through the dark spaces behind her. With the gun still pointed at his head, she changed her position and surveilled the woodland area around her. Everything was quiet and there was no indication of anyone being there.

"Move over there, against the tree," she instructed, keeping her gun aimed at his head. "Slowly!"

He did as she instructed.

Watching her back and keeping one eye on her surrounds, she leaned in to study his face once more.

"Where were you going to take me?" Her eyes were intense and intimidating.

"Who says *I* was taking you anywhere?"

He was as dumb as he looked, she thought, having tricked him into confirming he was waiting for someone. She circled him, slowly changing her stance to stay vigilant.

"I wonder what Mad Dog will do to you when I tell him you betrayed him."

Her words had him instantly tense up.

"You know, he did rip out a man's throat once. The guy bled out on his floor," she fibbed.

Zeus shuffled nervously.

"And that was just one of the Pythons." She referenced one of the other gangs in the area. "I don't even want to imagine what he'll do to someone he called a friend. Someone he thought he could trust."

"I'm not a traitor. I'd never betray my gang."

"Yet, here you are, Zeus, ready to share a bounty with Ludwig."

"I don't make deals with the devil. That man is a snake."

Again, Zeus stupidly revealed his hand.

But the disclosure left Jorja uneasy. If he hadn't struck a deal with Ludwig, then it meant only one thing. Züber was not involved. She had already suspected as much when Zeus let slip how much money he would get for capturing her.

"I should just call Mad Dog and tell him what a traitor you are." She slipped her hand inside her jacket pocket.

"No! Don't!" Zeus stopped her.

"You're a traitor, Zeus. You betrayed Mad Dog and he should know he has a mole in his business."

"You can't tell him, please! I'm sorry, okay? My family, they're all back in Jamaica, my sisters, my mum, they're all depending on me. Mad Dog will kill me and we will lose our house and the system will take my sisters."

Jorja had him right where she wanted him.

"Who hired you, Zeus?"

He wrestled with his answer and once again Jorja's hand slipped inside her pocket to pull out her phone.

"Okay, okay, I'll tell you. Just don't call Mad Dog, please!"

"I'm listening."

"Some Russian guy. He put the word out down at the corner shop about a week or so ago. When I called him up, he said he'd pay double if I got you before some guy called Uber or something got you."

"Züber."

"Yes, that's it. I told him I didn't know who that guy was but that it didn't matter because I already had you."

"That's who you were on the phone with, back at the flat," she instantly recalled.

He nodded. "I called him to say I found you."

"And? Where were you meeting him?"

"I was supposed to take you over that way, to the middle of the woods. There's a brook running past a bench. I had to tie you to the bench and leave you there. He said he'd leave the money under the seat by daybreak."

Jorja was quiet as she searched for a solution.

"How far is it from here?"

"Not far, maybe another fifty yards."

"I should just tie you to this tree and have Mad Dog come get you," she said, suddenly struggling with what to do.

"No, please, my sister, she's only twelve. She needs me."

Jorja couldn't think straight. She had no reason to doubt that the Russian man he spoke of was linked to Artem Sokolov. Not many Russian-speaking people could afford that big a bounty. It would have taken him no effort at all to find out that there were only a few people in the UK who could produce quality fake identities to help her hide from him, and Mad Dog was one of them. Putting the word out on the streets was a smart move.

She stared at Zeus where he awaited his fate. His eyes were pleading and she almost felt sorry for him. She thought of using Zeus and letting him carry out his plan.

That way Sokolov's men would take her straight to him and it would save her the effort of getting into his house. Or she could continue with her own plans and hunt down the lesser of the two evils first—Gustav Züber. Once he was out of the way, she could go after Sokolov.

She circled round to the other side of the tree until she stood just behind Zeus's right shoulder.

"Get up," she told him.

When he was standing, she wedged her gun firmly into his ribcage then spoke slowly next to his face.

"Did you ever stop to ask yourself why someone is prepared to pay such a high bounty for me?"

He shook his head.

"I'm not one to mess with, my friend. If you ever try to betray Mad Dog again I'll come for you myself, got it?"

Zeus nodded.

"You're going to go back to Mad Dog and tell him you lost me, that I got away from you. Then you're going to call your family and tell them you love them. Let this be the last stupid thing you ever do to Mad Dog or you will never see your family again."

She let the threat sink in.

"Now get out of here before I change my mind."

Zeus didn't waste any time and spun around almost instantly, darting back through the trees toward the commune.

CHAPTER TWENTY

When he was gone, Jorja was still wrestling over what to do. She stood in silence and gazed up into the darkness between the tall trees. Something was niggling at her but she just couldn't put her finger on it. Why would Sokolov offer a double bounty for her capture? Why not just let Züber do the dirty work, kill her, and take the fall for it? Surely it would save Sokolov from getting blood on his hands and running the risk of ruining his political reputation if he was caught?

As she tried to unravel the myriad questions that now flooded her mind, a twig snapped from somewhere behind her. She spun round in alarm, instantly annoyed with herself for once again dropping her guard. With her gun pointed at the bush the noise had come from, she waited, searching the dark space between the branches. Another noise came from behind the thick shrubs next to it. Her body tensed as she tried to steady her heartbeat that now pulsed uncontrollably in her chest. Expecting Sokolov's men to pounce on her at any moment she flexed her now sweaty palms around her gun's grip. She knew firsthand how dangerous Sokolov was. She had heard the screams that echoed from his house when she was there once. To this day, they were all too vividly etched in her mind. She shoved the memory aside and focused on the bushes once more.

When her body was ready to take action, ready to shoot at anyone who came out of those bushes, when she thought she would explode with tension, a fox crawled out from the undergrowth and scuttled away into the dark woodland.

"Ugh, you little rascal!" she shouted after it.

Although relieved that it was only a fox, the sobering experience quickly prompted her to get out of there before she did land up getting caught.

Turning toward the leaf-covered ground that led her back into the woodland, she managed to find her way back across the open grassed park and onto the footpath between the dwellings. Her car was parked in the street on the other end of where the path would eventually end back at the commune. To get to it, she would need to cross through the courtyard and out the other side, and, unlike earlier, every money-grabbing hoodlum would've by now heard what she was worth. She would be like a sheep thrown to a pack of wolves. She paused briefly to gather

her thoughts. Moving around by stealth was what she'd once done for a living. She used to be the best. There was no reason why she couldn't do it again.

Aided by the dark shadows of the crisp night, Jorja didn't waste any time and she quickly moved between the first blocks of buildings. Her senses were on full alert, detecting every sight, smell, or sound around her. It was like riding a bicycle, she thought when she successfully moved toward the second block. In a dark corner beneath a set of stairs, low voices drifted on the icy breeze. She paused, planned her next move, then swiftly glided past them along the outside of the building.

It took no time at all to successfully navigate the final block of flats and she soon found herself nearing the street where she had parked her car. It was well past midnight and, much to her relief—and aid—the streets were dark and quiet. When she was certain she wasn't followed, she turned the corner and hurried toward her car.

SHE WAS TIRED as she neared Heathrow Airport. By now Andre would have already worked his magic online and secured a seat for her on the 7:40 a.m. flight to Geneva. She would use the few hours before daybreak to take a catnap in her car once she parked it at the airport, then sleep more on the plane, she decided. When she was almost at the airport turnoff, her cell phone rang. She tried getting her phone but couldn't reach her satchel that was in the passenger side footwell. She unclipped her seatbelt then leaned over to pick it up, placing her bag on the seat next to her. With one hand on the wheel, she buried her other hand inside her satchel. As she blindly searched and found her phone, she wondered who would be phoning her at this time of night, not liking the uneasy feeling that had already made it into her chest.

"Hello?"

"Jorja, it's me." Charles's voice sounded numb on the other end of the line. "Sorry to call you this late, but... it's Ewan. I didn't want to wait until morning. I thought you should know. He didn't make it." His voice dropped toward the end and Jorja found herself unable to respond.

"Hello? Jorja, you there?"

"Yes, I'm here." Her voice sounded strange even to her.

"Did you hear what I said? Ewan's gone, Jorja, he died."

A lump formed in her throat when she tried to answer him and it took everything in her to force it down.

"I... I don't understand. They said he was going to be fine. How did he... how could this be?"

The road blurred in front of her as the tears pooled in her eyes.

"I know, I know, I'm so sorry. We all thought he was in the clear but the doctor said several bone fragments had made it into his arteries. He removed as many as he could but one had already ruptured one of his blood vessels. They didn't catch it in time. Ewan had begun hemorrhaging while in recovery, after the second surgery. By the time they got to him, it was too late."

Jorja could hardly breathe as the news of Ewan's death sank in.

"I'm sorry, Jorja. I know how close you two were, but if it helps at all, he's at home with the Lord now."

Charlie's words angered her.

"You say that but how do you know, huh, Charlie? How do you even know Heaven exists, or God for that matter?"

The suppressed anger in her voice took Charlie by surprise but he answered her the only way he knew how.

"Do you believe he loved you, Jorja?"

His question stung and she sat up in defense, wiping her runny nose with the back of her hand.

"What's that got to do with him dying?"

"Just answer me. Do you believe he loved you?"

"Yes, of course. I know he loved me!"

She was shouting.

"How do you know? Did he ever tell you?"

"Once."

"Once, then how do you know that was true?"

"Because he expressed himself. I felt it when I was with him. What are you getting at?"

"Exactly, he *showed* you how much he cared about you. Every time you were together you could feel it, sense it, heck we all could, every time the two of you were together in the same room."

She started crying again, as she recalled several moments they had shared over the years.

"God's love for us is the same way. We feel it, sense it, see it, if we allow ourselves to. Ewan was a child of God, Jorja. He's in Heaven."

Her shoulders threatened to shake with the weight of her sadness but she reined herself in, desperate to keep her car on the road.

"Then why did God take him? Why let him be shot in the first place? Ewan was the kindest person I knew. He didn't deserve to die, not like this."

She was sobbing now, unable to hold it back any longer.

"God's ways aren't always known to us, Jorja, but we have to trust that he does know what he's doing. Sometimes he reveals it to us and his reasons become clear to us at some stage, sometimes not. I know it won't take the pain away but I am going to do everything in my power to catch the guy who did this. I give you my word. And when that day comes, I will make sure he goes to jail for what he's done."

Charlie's oath weighed heavily on her heart. She knew exactly who'd killed Ewan and she was going to make him pay for it.

When they ended the call Jorja was no longer crying. Tears had made way for blind rage, hatred even. Charlie's words about God rang in her head and she pushed them aside. It meant nothing. God could have prevented Ewan from getting shot, stopped him from dying, saved him. But he hadn't. He'd let him die a horrible death all alone in the hospital without her even getting the chance to say good-bye. So strong were the emotions that now flooded her body that she had lost all sense of her surroundings. Over-taken by rage, regret, and plans to take revenge for her dear friend, her foot stepped down harder on the accelerator. She sped toward the airport, determined to give his murderer exactly what he deserved.

Blinded by her goal to take revenge for everything Gustav Züber and Artem Sokolov had taken from her, Jorja didn't see the vehicle speeding toward her car until the headlights were on top of her, and it smashed into the driver's door next to her.

CHAPTER TWENTY-ONE

A million glass fragments exploded into her face moments before Jorja's body was flung to the left, then came smashing into the driver's side hard steel door. Pain ripped through her head for the briefest of moments as her body lifted off her seat and hung weightless in the car before she came crashing down onto the dashboard. Feeling like she was inside a washing machine being pummeled on all sides by concrete boxing gloves, she tumbled and tossed out of control inside the tight space. Barely conscious of her surroundings her body left the car then slammed face-first into thorny foliage before she flipped over and thudded onto her back. Unable to breathe much she lay still, willing her mind to catch up with what had just happened. As her thoughts became clearer and the dark sky above her head came into vision, she knew she had been in a car accident. At first, she thought she might have been the cause since she was so distracted by the news of Ewan's passing. But then she recalled the deliberate thrusts into the side of her car by a silver pickup truck that had followed the initial collision. Someone had intentionally run her off the road.

She coughed, tasting the metallic tang of blood in her mouth. Ejecting it out the side of her mouth she tried sitting up but couldn't. Something was trapping her legs. When she lifted her head to see, she saw her legs had been caught between the branches of a small tree that had twisted round her legs, trapping her. Further inspection revealed the tree had saved her from rolling down a steep hill toward several sharp boulders that lined the edges of a large piece of rural land. Heaving hard as her torso twisted to one side she tried to free one leg. Pain shot through her ribs and she could hardly breathe. Again, she tried, this time trying to free the other leg instead. It worked, but she was now upside down lying headfirst toward the large boulders at the foot of the cliffside. One slip of her still trapped leg and she would slide down into the rocks below.

And that was one fall she knew she would not survive.

Overhead a jumbo jet flew low, its powerful turbines vibrating throughout her body. The plane's positioning and direction of flight indicated that she was on the east side of the airport, which meant the runway was just on the other side of the land below her.

Steeling herself, she tightened her stomach muscles into a sit-up and reached toward the tree trunk, relying on every bit of muscle in her abdomen to pull her upright. But the attempt proved futile when pain ripped through her left arm the moment she tried to take hold of the tree. Cringing in agony, she collapsed onto her back and clutched her arm to her chest. Although not broken, her arm was severely sprained, rendering it entirely unusable. Tears welled in her eyes and a sense of utter hopelessness and fear overwhelmed her.

Another plane took off and roared overhead. She couldn't give up, she thought. She had to fight and do what she needed to do, now more than ever. For Ewan. For Ben. For herself.

Using her uninjured arm, she attempted to sit up again, reaching into a cross-body crunch to grab hold of the tree. When her fingers eventually curled around the young tree's nearly smooth stem she pulled her body toward it, hugging it for dear life when she finally managed to sit up. Blood smudged tears ran down her cheeks and she caught herself thanking God for his help. It puzzled her, surprised her even. Almost as if the action was on autopilot and came from somewhere deep within her. She knew she could have died, should have died. The tree had saved her life. As she took a moment to make sense of it all, she couldn't help being reminded of a sermon she'd once heard about the tree of life. In the beginning, God had given it to Adam and Eve in the Garden of Eden, representing man's dependence on God. Then, in the middle of the Bible, he reminded his people of the wisdom and guidance the tree of life offered. Until finally, in Revelation, God told his people that he restores lives through the same tree of life, by offering eternal life in Heaven through his Son, Jesus Christ.

She recalled the conversation she'd had with Charlie. If what he said was true, and Ewan was in Heaven, what about her? Where would she have gone if she had died?

Voices coming from somewhere behind her startled her into the present. It was dark and she couldn't see that far up the side of the hill. She listened. They were male voices. One was shouting something at the other, then a door slammed. Moments later a beam of light shone down the hill.

It was them! The men who'd run her off the road. It could have only been Ludwig and his gang. Andre had mentioned that his methods were ruthless.

Gripping the tree between her legs and leaning her shoulder against the stem, her healthy arm went to find her gun in her waistband. But it was gone. It must have fallen out during the accident. *Her passport!* The thought echoed in her mind. It was in her bag, in the car, along with a few staple tools she would need to get into Züber's estate. Without her bag, she would not be able to get into his property, much less onto her flight for Geneva. Her eyes searched frantically for her car and almost immediately found it at the bottom of the hill where it had landed upside down against the boulders. Between where she was flung from the car and where the wreckage had come to a halt were several yards but it wasn't impossible to get to it —difficult, but not impossible. Using one arm only, she freed herself from the tree then used the slope to diagonally slide-shuffle down toward the car. From high above her, a flashlight beamed down in search of her until it settled on the wreck. Shielded only by the pitch-black darkness, she continued shuffling her way toward the car, briefly pausing only once when the flashlight's beam nearly exposed her. It wasn't a very bright light but it was strong enough for them to discover her. Adrenaline pumped violently through her body, numbing the pain in its wake. The gun was no longer of concern—she would have had to leave her gun behind in any event. All she needed to do was grab her bag and make a run for it across the acreage. Once she got to the airport, she would be safe. She had a passport and a valid ticket, that's all she needed.

But, in the distance behind her, at the top of the hillside, loose stones noisily rolled down, soon followed by more. The closer she came to the car the closer the tumbling stones rolled toward her, evidence that the men were climbing down to the car. She increased her speed, risking life and limb to get there first. If they caught up with her now they would finish the job and kill her, using the accident as the perfect cover-up. Her legs scraped across the rough terrain, slicing into her bottom and healthy hand along the way.

But she was almost there.

Mere yards away from the upside-down car a bullet smashed into the ground somewhere behind and to her left. It was close, too close.

Another exploded against the car.

Then another, directly behind her.

She was on her feet now, deciding to leap the final yard to the car. The men yelled at each other, the urgency of threat in their voices. One yelled to hit the car so it would explode, the other yelled not to do it. He was clearly the smarter of the two knowing that the bullets would foil their plan to make it look like an accident. Using their arguing to her advantage, Jorja lunged toward the hole in the front of the car where the windshield once was. Once inside the car wreck, crawling on her knees and one hand, she searched for the small satchel that had been next to her on the passenger seat at the time of the accident.

Her search turned up empty.

Further up along the dark slope the men's feet came thundering toward her. She was running out of time.

But it wouldn't be the first time in her life that Jorja came close to being nearly caught. She could handle pressure.

With her wits about her, calm and fully present in the moment, her eyes focused on the dark corners between the seats above her head. Then she spotted it. One of the satchel's straps dangled from behind the brake pedal. The satchel was pinned between the pedals and the floor. Her heart leaped in her chest as she moved to retrieve it.

But, in the shadows of the night that surrounded her, she had underestimated the men's distance from the car, and she had run out of time.

CHAPTER TWENTY-TWO

A strong hand grabbed her hair, sending powerful ripples of pain into her skull. The more she fought to loosen his grip on her locks, the more unbearable the agony was that tore into her scalp. Ignoring the suffering from her injured arm, she tried grabbing something to fight him off, cutting her hands on the shards of shattered glass in the process.

"Stop fighting it, you cow!" the man shouted, followed by a word used to describe a female dog along with several other unsavories she hadn't heard in a very long time.

Her cut fingers settled onto a large piece of the windscreen and she didn't hesitate to wrap her fingers around it, numbing herself against the pain as the sharp edges sliced into her flesh. With the sharpest end pointing outward, she thrust her hand back and over her head, jamming the piece of glass into her attacker's arm, enduring the pain as the force of it simultaneously sliced into her hand. He yelled, then let go of her hair and cursed her in the process. Desperate to get away from him she turned onto her back and drove her feet hard against his chest, flinging him onto his back and away from her and the car.

Once again, her hand reached for her satchel, this time gripping on with all her might. She flung one of the straps over her head and left the bag hanging around her neck like a necklace. Climbing over to the rear of the car was her only option for escape, something which proved harder than she'd expected since the car stood vertically, tail end up, against the high wall formed by the boulders. She had underestimated its height earlier from where she was wedged in the tree halfway down the hill and she slid back down toward the front of the car. The second attacker's hands clawed at her feet as he now reached in through one of the side windows. But she was quicker, slamming her heel down on one of his hands when he came too close.

Once more, she crawled toward the rear of the car; her knees and feet fighting hard not to slip on the glass and cause her to slide back down again. She caught hold of one of the safety belts, twirled it around her hand and wrist, then used it to pull herself up toward the rear windshield. Her sprained arm ached under the strain of being forced to use it to punch through the shattered window to create a hole big enough for her to climb through. When one last blow against the pane rendered it broken and released a shower of glass atop her head, she heaved herself out of the back window and over the trunk of the car. Still dangling from the seatbelt, her feet searched for a stable footing. Only once her feet found a safe gap between the boulders did she let go of the safety belt and climb down to the soft green grass below.

Turning briefly she glanced back to assess her enemy's position, thankful that neither of the men were in sight. There wasn't a moment to waste and she ran toward the airport as fast as her legs were able to carry her. It had started to rain and the cold, wet moisture against her skin proved to be more soothing than hindering. Without stopping, she pushed her now drenched hair out of her eyes, sweeping it back over her head. Blood-soaked rainwater ran into her eyes, blurring her vision so she could hardly see her way.

But she kept running. Faster, harder, pushing with every ounce of energy she had left in her through the knee-high grassland toward her freedom.

She allowed herself to look back only once, just to be certain she had escaped them and relieved to learn they hadn't followed her. But as she well knew, these men were not the type to give up that easily. They were most likely already making their way to the other end of the stretch of land. So she kept running, pushing her body to its maximum to get to the airport first. Once again, it was a race against time, and time was not on her side.

But as with all things in life, time soon passed and delivered her to the edge of the land where she was greeted by a high fence. On the other side of the fence, were several aircraft hangars—most of them shut apart from one that she could see.

Her body ached in more places than she cared to remember so she took a minute to catch her breath and rest. Using the rain to wash away the multitude of cuts on her face and hands she soon felt revived enough to continue.

The fence towered above her. She could try to climb it, she thought, albeit without full mobility. It seemed her only option and worth the effort. Eager to get to the safety of the airport she reached to take hold of the fence then snatched her hand back when it came mere inches away from the fence. She had instantly felt the static emanate from it, amplified by the rain. The fence was electrified.

Relieved to have stopped in time, she told herself that she'd come too close for comfort and had best be more careful in future. Searching for another way into the airport, she let her eyes trail up and down the fence in all directions, hoping to find any openings, gates, anything. But there were none. She could short the fence but that would most likely trigger an alarm and have airport security there within a few minutes. While she pondered her options, she concluded that shorting the fence might be her only option and that a few minutes were all she needed. Searching her bag for something that would suit to break the current, her hands found something else instead. Something that would not require her to blow the charger and allow her to proceed undetected.

With newfound enthusiasm as an idea took shape in her head, she retrieved a sturdy, red, zip pouch no bigger than her hand. She had forgotten that she had reasoned it might come in handy and had tossed it into her satchel just before she left home. From it, she took out an insulator cable and carefully attached it to the fence, creating a parallel bridging connection around a section of the fence. When she had finished, her hand disappeared inside her satchel once again to find a multitool, which she quickly used to sever the fence. Thrilled that one of her most tried and trusted methods of circumventing an alarm had worked, it took no time at all for her to clamber through the fence and make her way toward the hangars.

If she were to avoid suspicion and have any chance of boarding the airplane without any trouble, she would have to somehow clean up and make herself presentable. With any luck, there might be at least a tee shirt in one of the hangars.

As she neared the hangars, she proceeded with caution. Everything was quiet apart from one which had its doors open wide. She spotted activity coming from inside and backed into the shadows behind a small stationary food delivery truck. The vehicle had no driver and from her viewpoint, she could see into the hangar. A light shone brightly out onto the tarmac in front of the hangar and soon she heard several voices talking inside.

Moving two steps closer, she could now see four flight crew members step inside the small private aircraft. At the rear of the plane, there was a woman with a computer tablet, checking off boxes as a man in a gray overall loaded them into the aircraft. Either one of them would spot her running by to the next hangar, a chance she wasn't prepared to take. Glancing at her surroundings, she moved around the back of the food truck, hoping to be able to sneak around the back of the hangar where she would hopefully be able to get to the next one that appeared dark and unoccupied. With her body snug against the aircraft building's outer walls, she quickly made her way around the back where she found the rear entrance door closed. It had worked and her mission proved successful.

When she reached the second hangar's rear door, she noticed a single surveillance camera in the crook of the canopy above the door. It was a hard-wired camera and moved horizontally every few seconds, seemingly automatically. She would have to be quick to disable it, even quicker once she was inside. There was no doubt in her mind that she'd have eight minutes at the most to find what she was looking for and to get out before the response team arrived.

Nerves settled inside her throat. She hadn't done this in two decades and the possibility of her messing up was huge. But she had no other option. She had to finish what she'd started and not let Züber, Sokolov, or anyone else get away with what they'd done to Myles and now Ewan.

CHAPTER TWENTY-THREE

A nger welled up deep inside her once again and injected newfound courage and purpose into her mission.

With her multitool in hand, she hung back out of sight until the camera's lens faced away from her. When it was time, she quietly sneaked over and clipped the wire connection to disable the camera.

Next, she would have to bypass the electronic lock of the door without tripping the alarm. The red 'activated' light beamed into the darkness. She recognized the model. It was one she had dealt with hundreds of times, so she quickly went to work, once more reaching into her bag of tricks. She moved swiftly with a practiced hand she didn't realize she still had and inserted the USB end of a radio frequency identification device (RFID) into the portal of her iPhone, which had thankfully remained intact and was securely zipped inside her jacket's pocket. Holding the other end of the device against the electronic lock, her thumb found the app on her phone, and in less than ten seconds the RFID overrode the lock and the door sprang open.

Once inside she hesitated briefly at the door, first making sure that she was alone. To her right, a strong beam of moonlight broke through the clouds and partially lit up the front of the hangar through two large windows that sat at the top of each of the large hangar doors. On a clear night, it would have exposed her, but the gentle rain outside provided a cloudy cloak that allowed just enough light for her to see inside the large open space. When she knew she was safe, she ran toward the office to the left of her.

The door had been left open and she entered the partitioned space with ease. Her first instinct to look behind the door proved fruitful and she instantly spotted a dark green baseball cap dangling from a hook on the door. It was a start but not nearly enough to help disguise her. Her tee shirt was soaked with blood—that would be the first item of clothing she would have to replace. In the far corner, a single tan-colored locker stood in the corner and she hurried over, noisily yanking the door open in her haste. The flimsy metal echoed loudly through the space but she dared not stop. Time was running out. In the back of the locker, she found a scrunched-up blue and white men's shirt, looking as if a messy teenager had tossed it inside.

She snatched it up and tucked it under one arm, nearly fainting from the strong whiff of rank sweat it gave off which instantly permeated the small space. A packet of peanuts and a chocolate bar lay to one side, which she also quickly buried inside her satchel. She was starved and even though they were quite possibly as stale as the shirt, it was a chance she would need to take.

In the far distance, she heard tires screeching. They were at most a few minutes away. She was running out of time, fast. She slammed the locker shut then turned out of the office and into the adjacent bathroom. It was much cleaner than she'd expected and she yearned to take a shower in the single cubicle she spotted inside. But it would have to wait. Instead, she darted toward the wash-basin, splashed several handfuls of cold water over her face, then rinsed her lacerated hands under the tap before drying herself off with the white hand towel with red embroidered flowers that neatly hung from a hook next to her. To one side a matching cherry blossom red room fragrance stood proudly atop a pretty glass bowl of potpourri—no doubt the work of a woman, she thought when she sprayed a generous amount of the fragranced liquid all over the tee shirt.

Outside, a car door slammed shut followed by two more doors before a dog barked loudly into the early morning air. Changing shirts would have to wait, for now. They were out front, by the main doors, but would most certainly already be making their way to the rear entrance door since this was where the camera feed was cut. Dumping the towel in a nearby garbage bin, Jorja searched for another way out but didn't find any. Her eyes settled on the single executive jet in the center of the hangar and she wasted no time. She would hide inside, take her chances. Bolting across the squeaky floor the shiny black aircraft's door latch was just outside her reach and stretching to grab hold of it sent new tremors of pain into her ribcage. The armed response team's feet shuffled noisily just outside the hangar door and she reached up once more. The door dropped open and she forced the hydraulics down to speed up the process. Once inside, she moved quickly to shut the door then dashed swiftly between the cabin windows, dropping down the blinds. Apart from the cockpit and the bathroom, there weren't many places to hide. Out of time and out of options, she moved toward the cockpit and stopped just outside when she noticed a wall of cupboards. She yanked one open and found a black hostess dress, neatly pressed inside the dry cleaner's plastic covering.

"I guess it's time for plan B," she whispered.

Wasting no time at all as the response team's feet squeaked on the floor inside the hangar, she changed into the uniform, fumbling to tie the dark green neckerchief with one hand. In a translucent cosmetic bag, she found a compact powder and a bright red lipstick. The top flipped open under her thumb to expose her badly lacerated face in the tiny mirror. Just as well she'd found the make-up, she thought. There would have been no way on earth she would get away with the ruse with her face looking like that. Holding the compact with her injured arm her other hand moved quickly to apply the make-up. It was at least two shades too dark but it did the trick and she dabbed some on the back of her hands where the cuts were raw and threatened to give her away. She had just finished and was applying the red lipstick when the aircraft's door latch alerted her to their arrival. She smoothed back her hair and stuffed her clothes inside the closet just as a guard stepped aboard the plane, his hands ready on his truncheon.

"Now, aren't you the early bird this morning," she said sounding chirpy. "I wasn't expecting you for at least another hour. I really should speak to Barry about getting the schedule right. The young kids of today—"

"Excuse me, ma'am, is everything all right?" The man cut her short, his eyes darting up and down the cabin.

"What on earth do you mean? Of course, I'm all right. Why do you ask?"

"You sure?"

She looked at him inquiringly, bluffing her way through her con.

"Yes, I am sure. Why wouldn't I be? I've been doing this job for nearly twenty years now. I am more than capable of prepping the plane before take-off."

"No, I, sorry, ma'am, I didn't mean to imply you were

incompetent. I meant to ask if you are safe, if you've heard or seen anyone break into the hangar."

"Break in? What are you saying? I have been here since four a.m. and I assure you, I would have known if someone broke in. Our client likes everything just so before she flies anywhere so I have to be extra careful not to miss anything."

The man hesitated.

"Do you mind if I take a look around?"

"Isn't that what you are supposed to do before every take-off? I would've thought Barry would check that you know the protocol, but no," she said, pretending to blame a co-worker.

"Barry didn't call us, ma'am. We received an alert on the surveillance camera at the rear entrance."

"Oh, so you're not here to do the checks then?"

"No ma'am that must be a different division."

Jorja knew he wouldn't have a different answer since she had made it all up, but she needed to play the part out, so she continued.

"Well, in that case, perhaps you wouldn't mind giving me a lift back to Terminal 2, please? I need to just check in with my supervisor."

The guard had already walked through the small space to the rear of the plane and made his way back to where Jorja stood waiting in the nose of the plane, her hands concealed beneath an in-flight blanket.

"Certainly, ma'am, ready when you are."

"Wonderful, let me grab my bag and my coat, I'm right behind you."

She reached into the closet and replaced the blanket with her jacket and satchel then turned toward him, curving her newly painted red lips into a friendly smile.

Not only had her deception worked, but it had worked so well that she'd pulled off a free ride into the airport.

CHAPTER TWENTY-FOUR

From the window of his home office in Kazan, Russia, Artem Sokolov watched his two young children play in his extensive garden below. His private estate stretched along the banks of the Volga River, a home he had acquired solely because of the privacy and security it offered. At only fifty-five years of age, he was one of Russia's wealthiest business oligarchs, with a net worth of nearly forty billion US dollars. The younger of two children, his parents had worked in the local steel mills and lived off government food stamps for most of his life. But when his older sister strategically married a local wealthy businessman, she funded his university studies in engineering. He soon worked his way up the ladder in the steel industry and with his new brother-in-law's influence in the business world, Sokolov quickly secured a business loan with which he bought his first small steel plant. Once Boris

Yeltsin introduced his privatization program, it changed the trajectory of his life almost overnight and he became one of the youngest oligarchs in Russia. Since then, he has snapped up several more steel plants across Russia and the US, building his empire alongside politicians, billionaires, and even presidents.

He was twice divorced and had three children—two with his first wife, and the youngest with his second. For reasons mostly based around tax and diversifying his wealth, he bought them each a home—one in London, England, the other in Geneva, Switzerland. For two weeks of the year, he would have his kids fly in to visit with him in Russia before they returned to their respective homes and school, a life he preferred not only because his kids could get a better education, but also to keep them all from seeing what lengths he often had to go to in order to get what he wanted. And, as with most wealthy businessmen in Russia, such lengths meant that the lines were often crossed between good and evil. Although not a member of any Russian organizations or mobs, he had learned early on that it was most beneficial to him if he had a few crooked politicians and the KGB in his pocket. Such relationships had saved him a great many times over his career.

With his youngest child having left for London the day before, he had freed his day to enjoy a picnic with his remaining two children on their final day with him. At least, that was the plan.

He emptied a glass of Beluga vodka and slammed the empty glass on the desk, spitting the last few drops of alcohol from the corners of his mouth as he spoke.

"I thought I gave you strict instructions not to interrupt me today, Thomas. Yet, here I am, in my office watching my children enjoy the sunshine on their own with you yapping in my ears. This had better be good news, you hear me?" He admonished his head of operations who had interrupted their picnic.

"Forgive me, Mr. Sokolov, but this couldn't wait. I thought you'd want to know this right away," the much younger British native replied.

"Well, what is it?"

"Sergei's efforts to kill the target failed, sir."

Artem's deep-set eyes darkened under his heavy black brows as disapproval threatened behind them. He walked over to his desk and went to stand behind it, leaning his body on his fists atop his desk as he looked sternly at Thomas.

"What do you mean 'failed'?"

"He lost her after she left the roadside hotel but he caught up with her again near the National Gallery, but then apparently she just vanished into thin air."

Artem slammed a fist on the brown leather padding of his walnut desk.

"How hard could it be to catch this woman? She is not some secret spy or something. It's ridiculous!"

"There's more, sir." The young man's large Adam's

apple nervously moved up and down his throat as he mustered the courage to share what came next.

"It looks like Züber's men got to her first."

Artem let out a string of Russian expletives. His already dark eyes were now nearly pitch-black as he stared at the young man's face.

"Explain," Artem said, his voice cold, demanding, and without emotion.

"My informants tell me Züber hired one of the most dangerous gangs in South London—a guy by the name of—"

"I don't care about his name! Do they have her, yes or no?"

"No, they don't, sir. They tried to kill her it seems, but she escaped them, twice."

Thomas's mobile phone pinged and, at the risk of being lambasted further he sneaked a look. His face instantly lit up.

"Sergei found her, sir! She's at the airport, due to board a plane to Geneva. Seems she is traveling with a false passport. He managed to get onto the same flight as her and they are due to arrive in a couple of hours. By the looks of it, she was pretty banged up. Whatever they did to her, she survived. It's insane. This woman's got nine lives."

The man in his early thirties let out a relieved giggle as his shoulders relaxed and color slowly returned to his face. He had worked for Artem for ten years and had witnessed himself how ruthless his boss could be. As good as he was at his job, he also knew Artem wouldn't hesitate to get rid of him if he so much as put a foot wrong, especially with something as important as this. Artem had made it his mission to hunt Georgina down for a couple of decades now and nothing would stop him from unleashing years of anger toward her. As far as he knew, people who crossed Artem Sokolov never lived to tell the tale.

"So the vixen's off to Geneva, is she?" Artem had his back to Thomas where he stared out his window again.

"Yes, sir. Why do you think she is planning to go to see Züber? They couldn't possibly be back in business again."

Artem turned to face him with a glowering look.

"Sometimes you say the stupidest things, Thomas. Why would she be back in business with him if he has sent half of England's gangsters after her, huh? He has a score to settle with her as much as I do."

"Of course, sir." Thomas's face flushed with embarrassment.

Artem dropped into his leather president's chair and, resting his elbows on the armrests, fanned the tips of his fingers together under his chin.

"Our little devil-woman is going to confront him. Knowing her, she thinks she can go after him. Possibly kill him before he kills her. And since we know how smart she is, she's probably already figured out that we've been watching her."

"You don't think she's coming for us next, do you, sir?"

"I wouldn't put it past her, but not if we surprise her

and get to her first. Call Sergei. Tell him there's a change of plan. I want him to bring both of them to me instead, alive."

Thomas's eyes stretched open wide and his voice broke as he asked, "You mean both Züber and Georgina? Here, alive?"

"Yes, Thomas, you heard me. I have waited long enough for this day to come and I would be an idiot to let Sergei rob me of the pleasure of seeing her die. I should experience the look in her eyes personally and now I will have the pleasure of watching both of them squirm when they beg for my forgiveness. I will kill both of them. The way I see it, it is double the pleasure. How do you English people always say? Two birds with one stone, huh? I can hardly wait."

"Sir, with respect, if we bring them here we run the risk of exposing you. Your entire reputation is on the line. If we are caught, here in Russia... sir, it's a huge risk. May I remind you that we have run out of collateral? I don't have anything left in the vault that is worth enough to get you off a double murder. I've had to use the Rembrandt to get you out of your last... indiscretion."

Artem Sokolov's eyes narrowed and he was instantly upright in front of the window again.

"You're right, Thomas. I am letting my hatred for those two swindlers cloud my judgment. It seems they have beaten me once again. If I have no bargaining chips left, I could lose it all. I can't do that to my children."

Thomas was suddenly next to him, his eyes glimmering with an idea.

"Not necessarily, sir. I think we can still do this."

Artem turned to face him.

"I'm listening?"

"Your house in Geneva, we can do it there."

"And risk the lives of my children? That's your grand plan? Absolutely not!"

"Hear me out, sir. We have the tunnels that run underneath the estate, the ones we found recently when we upgraded the west wing. I had my men look into it. Apparently, the Swiss loved their underground bunkers and tunnels, and the ones we found under your Geneva house date back to the Second World War. It was part of the Swiss Redoubt program implemented by the Swiss government, as a defense protocol in the event of a German invasion. They will serve as the ideal place to take both Georgina and Züber. It's airtight and not even she could escape from it. And being so deep underground, your ex-wife and children would be none the wiser."

Artem took a few moments to digest Thomas's suggestion. There were days the guy annoyed him with his naivety, but then there were days like this when his bright mind reminded him why he had kept him on his payroll all this time.

He smiled and placed his hands atop Thomas's shoulders, patting them in proud approval before he turned around to take in his children's happy faces again.

"It can work, but you've got to promise me you'll keep my children and their mother safe. I don't care what you have to do, but you keep them safe."

"You have my word, sir. I'll make the arrangements immediately."

Thomas turned to leave the room.

"One more thing, Thomas, make sure Sergei knows of our new plan and tell him, if he loses that woman again he's a dead man. We have one shot at this and I will not let anything or anyone mess this up. I've waited too long."

"I'll take care of it, sir. It will work. Actually, our timing could not be more perfect considering you could now take your kids home yourself. Your ex-wife won't suspect a thing and neither Züber nor Georgina will see us coming."

Artem's mouth pulled into a satisfying grin as he spoke again.

"Yes, it's the perfect plan. Finally, I have Züber and Georgina exactly where I want them and nothing will give me greater pleasure than to see them at my feet, pleading for me not to kill them."

CHAPTER TWENTY-FIVE

J orja settled into the nearly full plane and swept her eyes over the passengers. She might have made it there in one piece—barely—but it didn't mean she had shaken Züber's guys off her trail. And since Zeus had confessed Sokolov was also involved, she wasn't safe from his men either.

So, she kept one eye open, just in case, resting in the knowledge that, considering she had scarred both their faces during her escape, there would be no mistaking the men who tried to run her off the road. She would surely spot them among the passengers in a heartbeat.

Her body was bruised and ached all over, welcoming the plush cushioning of the first-class seat Andre had booked for her. Upgraded traveling wasn't a choice; it was a necessity and the only way she could get on and off a plane quickly. She had learned this very early on in her career and had used the airlines' VIP privileges to her advantage to escape many tight situations in the past.

As soon as the plane took off, she got up and walked toward the restroom where one passenger had just entered the small cubicle. This she had intentionally planned as a way to obtain a bird's-eye view of all the passengers in first class. She paid particular interest to the two men who flanked her. To the right of her seat was an older man whose expensive gold watch and off-white designer suit didn't fit the profile of a killer. His hands were shaking, possibly from Parkinson's, and he'd declined the glass of champagne upon arrival. As far as she could tell, he was not a threat.

The man to her left, however, she wasn't sure of. He was of average height, well dressed, and even though he had a certain charm about him, he looked nervous and was already on his second Scotch. Either this was his first time on a plane, or he was about to get married, but something did not quite add up.

He looked up at her, saw she was looking at him then quickly hid his face behind the in-flight magazine. Jorja's suspicions grew and she caught the attention of the flight crew member who was prepping the in-flight snacks at the station behind her.

"Excuse me, I know this is probably none of my business but the man seated in seat 2B, is he all right? He just seems on edge or something."

The young woman, roughly in her mid-twenties,

sneaked a peek from behind the half-drawn red curtain then replied with a smile.

"Oh, that's Rupert Pemberton. He's terrified of flying, poor soul."

Jorja relaxed.

"*The* Rupert Pemberton, from Pemberton and Lochton, the Queen's jewelry makers?"

She nodded with glee. "I know, right? He has meetings in Geneva at least twice a month. He is super embarrassed about it, bless him. But don't let it bother you, he'll settle down as soon as his meds kick in. Can I get you something?" She recoiled when her manager cast a watchful eye in her direction.

"No, I'm good thanks, just waiting for the loo."

"Well, I'll be sure to set down your tray if you haven't made it back to your seat by the time I pass it, and just shout if you need anything else, okay?"

Jorja nodded and slipped inside the small washroom as soon as it was free. Inside the cramped space, she relaxed her guard and told herself that she was probably just paranoid since she had not slept in days. She was on a plane for goodness sake. It's not like they would kill her mid-flight or anything.

Taking a deep breath, she adjusted the make-shift sling she had made for her arm from a silk scarf she had picked up from the Duty Free shop. She had also swapped out her stolen garb for a new pair of jeans and a pale blue tee shirt, disposing of the dress in the canteen waste bin before she boarded. Her wristwatch told her she had less than an hour before they landed, not nearly enough time for her to squeeze in a nap.

In the mirror in front of her, she studied the dark rings that had formed under her eyes. Deep red bruises had settled on her jaw and several small wounds threatened to rise to the surface from beneath the rushed make-up job in the hangar that was no longer nearly enough to conceal them. While she took advantage of the safety and solitude of the small in-flight washroom, she thought of Ewan and the circumstances under which he had died. That she wasn't there for him in his last moments, to say goodbye. She recalled his eyes looking up at her from where he was bleeding out on the floor in her gallery. Even while staring death in its face, his eyes were warm and reassuring. Thinking back now, Ewan had always made it about her, selflessly putting her needs before his in every situation, protecting her even at the cost of losing his life.

Guilt suddenly engulfed her and tears fell down her cheeks as she recalled the day he'd told her he loved her, that he would do anything to make her happy. She had known that he was in love with her months before, but as much as she wanted to love him back, she couldn't, not in the way he loved her. She had lost her heart to someone else long before Ewan came along, and now she would never see either of them again.

Jorja quietly wept for the first time since hearing of Ewan's passing. She mourned the loss of her dear friend who'd sacrificed everything. She mourned losing the only man she'd ever loved for a second time, this time for good. She cried for what her life had become, and for what it could never be. She had nothing and no one left. All she had left was the anger toward the men who had taken it all away. The men who had robbed her of ever having a normal life, from a future with Ben, from having any meaning to her life. She hated them with everything she had left in her.

And while her sadness slowly transformed into resentment and guilt over allowing them to get away with it for so long, the tears slowly dried up. When she finally stared into the mirror again, she saw nothing but bitterness, and all that remained were the streaks her tears had left behind in the make-up.

Lukewarm water ran from the tap and she splashed several cupped hands full of the soothing liquid on her face. She didn't care if the make-up washed off and revealed the scratches. She was done hiding. She was done pretending. Come what may, both Gustav Züber and Artem Sokolov will pay for what they'd done to her, for taking Ewan, for taking Ben.

And even if it were the last thing she would ever do on this earth, she would not let them go unpunished.

A GENTLE RAPPING at the door pulled her back into the present. She had completely lost track of time. Drying her face, she adjusted her hair and drew in a deep breath before she opened the door to exchange places with an uppity woman whose eyes looked daggers at her. Back in her seat, her thoughts continued to consume her mind as she tucked into the fresh chocolate croissant and orange juice the attendant had left for her. A smile settled on her face. It wasn't a smile of joy, rather a smile filled with self-satisfaction. Because for the first time in a very long while, she knew exactly what she needed to do to set herself free.

Twenty-four hours earlier, she had planned to make her way to the quaint guesthouse nestled on the banks of the lake. She and Ben had discovered it by accident one year when they got lost. The house was quiet and off the beaten path, accessible only by foot—if you knew where to find it. She had thought she would need to hide out there for a few days to strategize and plan her way into Züber's house with minimum risk. But now none of that mattered anymore. There wasn't a moment to spare. She didn't need to sleep, didn't need to recover. She had been at his house a thousand times before; he wasn't one to change anything. Gustav was an old dog who thought no one could teach him any new tricks. Even prison wouldn't have taken away his arrogance or obstinance. She had helped him with his security, found any loopholes that could put him and his art at risk. She knew his house like the back of her hand.

But he knew that.

Yes, he would know by now she was coming for him, but not how or where to expect it. She didn't care about his house or the few small pieces of art she was certain he kept there. Her plan included taking something far more important to him.

Allowing her eyes to drift to the full-page advert on the back cover of the in-flight magazine in front of her, she couldn't pass up on the opportunity that stared her in the face.

No matter how much she hated him, she couldn't kill him even if she wanted to. She wasn't a cold-blooded killer, nor would she ever be. But taking the only thing Gustav Züber had ever loved more than himself, that she could do. Prison was nothing compared to losing his entire fortune and all the precious art he had been hiding in plain sight for decades.

There was one place on earth he was too arrogant and proud to hide from the world. One place he did not want to conceal behind the smokescreen of his shell companies or fictitious collectors—it was what had given him credibility in the industry and he would never separate from it. It was the only place to which Züber attached his name, and seeing him go down during the biggest fine art gallery in Switzerland's annual private banquet, was all the revenge she could ever want. Twenty years ago she had kept one final ace up her sleeve, in the event the evidence she had leaked to the police wasn't enough.

Now the time had come for her to place the final card on the table. One that would expose him to the world and strip him of everything he owned, and it just so happened to be taking place that very evening.

There would be no stone left unturned and Gustav Züber's entire empire would come crumbling down, in front of the entire world for all to see.

CHAPTER TWENTY-SIX

Sneaking off the plane once she landed in Geneva was easier than she'd thought it would be. She remained alert, expecting Züber's men to have followed her onto the plane. But they hadn't.

Perhaps the injuries she'd inflicted upon them were worse than she'd thought, or maybe they decided half a million quid was not worth the effort anymore. Either way, she was relieved to have shaken them.

The thirty-something-year-old branch manager at the car rental company didn't hesitate to accept the hefty under-the-table cash bonus in exchange for giving her a complimentary car—since she didn't have time to obtain a fake credit card—an easy target once she'd noticed the congratulatory balloons and photos of a newborn all over his office. She knew very few new parents who didn't need extra funds after welcoming a baby so it turned out to be the perfect motivator.

She pointed the silver Renault Clio's nose in the direction of Balexert, one of the bigger shopping malls in the city. In order to access the safety deposit box in which she kept the tell-all memory stick, she would need to change back into the person she'd been when she acquired the box. She would also need a dress and fresh disguise to make it into the banquet undetected. Parking the car as close to the mall exit as possible, she kept a low profile, obscuring her face from any surveillance cameras with a dark gray wool fedora she'd nicked from a passing passenger in the car rental company's foyer, which she pulled low over her eyes. She had removed her arm from the scarf sling, resting it instead, inside her leather jacket's pocket to keep it still. She had done this a million times before so it should go off without a hitch, she thought, as she walked into a trendy hair accessories shop that displayed several good quality wigs in the window. Once inside she skimmed over the three-dozen wigs that sat perched on glass shelves, stopping when she spotted an ash-brown wig with hair that would hang below her shoulders. Pretending to read a text on her phone, she didn't look up when she slid the cash over to the young girl behind the counter.

Two doors down she picked up some fresh make-up— concealer that would provide proper coverage, mascara, and the bright red lipstick she'd worn in her Swiss passport photo.

Last on her list were two new outfits. One to look the part for the bank, and a second to wear to the banquet. It took hardly any time at all and she soon walked out of the shopping mall, filled with an old familiar feeling of excitement blended with a heavy dose of satisfaction. Thus far, everything was going according to plan. All she needed now was a place to get dressed.

She glanced at her watch. Six hours until the banquet, plenty of time to change twice and get to the bank. Finding a hotel was an obvious choice since there was only one hotel midway between the bank and the gallery.

When she reached the underground parking garage, shopping bags and plans firmly in hand, she noticed the rental car's passenger door was slightly ajar, as if someone hadn't properly closed it. Even from a healthy distance, she sensed immediate danger and quickly diverted toward the nearby elevator. Tension ripped at her insides as she jabbed the button repeatedly, keeping her head down.

Someone had found her.

The elevator doors finally opened and she was greeted with a giggling group of teenage girls who nearly bulldozed her to the floor when they got out of the lift. Attention was the last thing she needed and she hastily pushed her way past them and took cover in the corner. The main lobby was one floor up and once again, she jabbed her finger at the button to hurry the doors into closing.

But it was too late.

Two men stepped inside the elevator and she instantly recognized the smell of cheap liquor and sweat they emanated. They were the two men who'd driven her off the road—Ludwig and his hairy sidekick.

She kept her head low, her face hidden under her fedora, her back against the wall in the back of the elevator. Either they had not noticed it was her, or they were waiting for the doors to close first.

And her money was on the latter.

As the doors closed, she waited for them to make the first move and as predicted, it didn't take long for them to take action. Ludwig attacked first, spinning around with his arm lunging toward her stomach, a large switchblade in his hand. She was quick to step aside, dodging it by mere inches. Her hand folded around his wrist, twisting his arm to contort it behind his back. A split second later the switchblade was in her injured hand, shooting pangs of agony up her arm. Her healthy arm wrapped around Ludwig's thick neck, pinning him in a firm chokehold, the knife pressed firmly against his tattooed throat.

"Get her!" He yelled for his hairy sidekick to intervene, but Jorja had already manipulated the inexperienced bounty hunters back into the far corner.

As she waited for the elevator to hurry to the lobby so the doors would open behind her, Ludwig yelled out again. This time, his associate pulled a gun and tried to aim it at her face over Ludwig's shoulder.

"Save it, unless you want to see his throat slit," Jorja threatened, forcing the sharp blade deeper into Ludwig's flesh until blood trickled from beneath it.

The man's eyes darted nervously back and forth between his boss' and her, the gun now trembling in his hand.

"Grow some, you coward. Shoot her!" Ludwig kept yelling.

The man zeroed in, as best he could under the nervous tension that threatened his aim. His forefinger moved to press the trigger, pausing when Jorja suddenly changed position and forced him off focus.

"Drop the gun, man. You know you will miss and hit his head instead of mine. His gang will hunt you down for killing him and you know it."

She was buying time, but messing with the shooter's head was her only option.

"No! You let him go! I'm the one with a gun, not you!" he made a pathetic attempt to threaten her.

She ignored it, reciprocating with one of her own.

"Last chance, my friend." Once more she pressed the blade deeper into Ludwig's throat.

She knew she had already won when moments later the automated elevator voice announced their arrival in the lobby.

With her opponent distracted by the imminent opening of the doors, she drove Ludwig to the ground by jamming her foot into the back of his knee. As he fell groaning to the floor, she sliced the blade over the hairy guy's arm, forcing him to drop the gun onto the floor. It took all of two seconds to finish them off. First, she planted a firm kick across Ludwig's face, then broke the hairy guy's nose with her fist, rendering both unconscious on the floor just as the doors opened.

AN HOUR later Jorja was already on foot to the Schweitzer Bank. Using the new identity Andre had created for her, she had successfully checked into the hotel and selected a room on the third floor, closest to one of the fire escapes. It did not hurt to be overly cautious at this point. She glanced at her watch. If she encountered any further delays she was at risk of blowing her entire mission, so she increased her pace, grateful for the painkillers she'd managed to get from the boutique shop in the hotel lobby.

Dressed in a tailored navy pantsuit, she looked every bit the part of a wealthy woman. Beneath her matching fedora, her long ash-brown wig fell over her shoulders, its rich tones emphasizing her cherry red lips that matched her six-inch heels. With the posture and attitude of a powerful woman who had the world at her fingertips, she entered the bank. In keeping with her disguise, she enquired about her safety deposit box in fluent French. Nerves threatened beneath her calm exterior as she entered the vault, suddenly doubting if she would recall the digital combination.

But she did, with ease, since it was a combination of her and Ben's birthdates. The box sprang open and she lifted the armor-proof lid. When her eyes fell on the contents of the box, her heart plunged into her stomach and instantly spoiled her victory. Her fingers moved to pick up the black velvet box. She had forgotten it was in there. The small square container nestled into the palm of her hand sent mixed sensations of regret and sadness through her body. Fighting the urge to give in to the wave of tears that threatened behind her eyelashes, she snapped the lid open. Tucked between red satin folds the two-carat yellow diamond engagement ring glistened under the room's sharp lights. Memories of Ben's proposal flooded her mind, sending her heart to pulse out of control in her throat.

She snapped the box shut and dropped it back into the steel box as if it had just bitten her finger, annoyed for allowing her heart to run away with her.

Forcing her mind—and heart—back to more impor-tant matters at hand, she dabbed the lonely tear that had settled on her lower lid with two fingertips and focused instead on Gustav's face, reminding herself that he was the reason she would never be able to wear Ben's ring again. Controlled and back in the grip of her hatred toward her target, she reached in and took the memory stick from the box, tucking it inside her bustier.

"Desperate times call for desperate measures," she said under her breath as she slipped the security box back in its place and moved to exit the building.

But in the slightest of instants when she least expected it, everything changed the moment she stepped out of the bank and onto the cobbled curb.

Flanked by Ludwig and his hairy wingman, the hard steel points of two guns wedged deep into her ribcage on both sides of her body.

CHAPTER TWENTY-SEVEN

L udwig's big-knuckled hand clamped down on Jorja's bicep. His breath reeked of cheap beer and garlic, a smell that nearly made her hurl right there on the curb. His sidekick's podgy fingers were a tad more forgiving, something she was grateful for since he had her by her bad arm.

"Walk," Ludwig said through gritted teeth when she slowed down too much.

"I'm happy to exchange my six-inch heels for your boots if you like then we can see how fast you walk on these cobbled sidewalks," she replied with sarcasm.

He grunted in response and shoved the gun deeper between her ribs.

"Of course, you could always tell me where you're taking me then I can meet you there and save us all a lot of trouble."

"Shut up and walk before I put a bullet through you."

She scoffed.

"Ah, yes, that's precisely what you should do if you're abducting someone in the middle of a foreign city." She raised her voice intentionally on the abduction part and it made him grip her arm harder.

"I told you to shut your trap, woman," he said leaving a puff of his foul-smelling breath in her face.

"Nice nose job, by the way," she said, ignoring his warning once again.

She was riling him up on purpose, she wanted him to lose his cool since she was fully aware he wouldn't create a scene—or kill her—on a busy sidewalk. More than that, she already knew where they were taking her and it didn't matter at this point. Sure, her plot to expose Züber would not be quite as impactful or gratifying as doing it at his biggest fundraising gala in front of all his esteemed colleagues, but she would expose him, nonetheless. All it would take was to find a computer and send the files to the FBI. She would simply bypass his security and escape, no big deal.

AT THE END of the block, they ushered her into a quieter street where a stratus blue Volvo sedan was already parked up and waiting for them. As they came closer, she could see the back of a man's head where he was seated in the driver's seat. He popped the trunk as they reached the car.

Ludwig's meaty hand shoved her against the rear of the car causing her hat to fall on the ground next to her feet.

"Get in."

His hairy sidekick followed suit, prodding her side with his gun.

"Come now, fellows. This is no way to treat a lady. I promise I won't bite if I sit next to you on the back seat."

He clenched down hard on his jaw, pushing the muscles in the sides of his cheeks to the surface.

"Quit playing games, woman, and get in the trunk before I smash that pretty little face of yours in."

Her heart pounded against her chest and she took a deep breath, steeling herself for a fight.

She seized the moment and thrust her forehead into his already broken nose. He groaned in pain and instantly let go of her arm.

The hairy man's arm closed over the back of her neck, forcing her head forward into the trunk of the car. His podgy thumb drove hard into the soft flesh behind her ear while his stocky body heaved on top of her back. But she fought back as hard as she could, driving her fist into his groin.

He let go, and she heard the driver's side door open.

To her right Ludwig had already recovered and drove his fist into her right kidney.

She doubled over, gasping for breath.

From somewhere behind her a soft rag closed over her mouth.

A sweet-smelling odor seeped into her nostrils before the sweet taste settled on her tongue.

The car became blurry. Then everything spun around her.

The sweet scent drove into her legs. Her knees gave way.

Then everything went black.

SOFT LIGHT FLICKERED from behind her heavy eyelids as she tried forcing them open. Disorientated, her mind scrambled to make sense of her surroundings. Her body felt lethargic, her tongue thick and furry. As she lifted her head to take it all in, pain stabbed behind her eyes and caused her to flinch, forcing her to pause for a moment to adjust to the light. The sweet taste in her mouth had transformed to an intensely sharp sensation that scratched at the back of her tongue and she wished she had some water to rid her mouth of the dryness.

Shoving the discomfort aside she homed in on her vision, forcing her eyes to penetrate the orange glow that surrounded her. The room looked warm and inviting and wasn't what she had expected to see after having been abducted. It was dignified, welcoming even. She was seated in the center of the room, bound to a carved vintage oak chair. Thick ropes ran around the back of the chair, and her waist and torso, keeping her fastened in place atop the dark leather seat.

Her feet were tied at her ankles, mirroring the same thick rope around the carved legs of the chair. Running across a large section of the floor underneath the chair and her feet was a hunter's green and gold Persian rug. She didn't recognize it. Confusion set in at the back of her mind. Perhaps Ludwig wasn't working for Gustav after all. Perhaps she had assumed wrong and it wasn't even Gustav who'd been after her to begin with. Through hazy eyes, she took in the seventeenth-century carved oak dining table, surrounded by seven chairs matching the one she was seated on. To her right, a fire roared in an open fireplace framed by an ornate marble mantelpiece with two lions carved into the marble on either side. A companion set of antique brass pokers dangled from a nearby rotary and she made a mental note that they would serve well as weapons should she need them later.

She twisted as much of her body as the ropes' tension would allow, looking over her shoulders to take in the rest of the space. The room was large and sparsely furnished, taken up mostly with the dining table and a few button-threaded wingback chairs positioned in front of a large window that had a direct view onto a lake. Concluding that it must be Lake Geneva, she tried making sense of her exact location but the sun had already started to set behind the tall trees that flanked the house on both sides.

"Hello?" she called, not expecting anyone to answer since the house was deathly silent. She listened nonetheless, hearing nothing but the calm flickering sounds of the fire.

When she was certain no one was around, she wriggled trying to free herself from the ropes but found it futile. She heaved the chair upward, willing it to move closer to the fireplace. If she could grab hold of one of the pokers, she might be able to cut through the ropes. The chair's legs stuck to the piles in the carpet, making it difficult for her to slide across the floor. Dull thumps echoed throughout the room instead and she silently prayed that no one would hear her.

But the wishful thought was soon to be just that when Gustav Züber's voice brought her to a standstill.

"Well, well, well, it seems my long-lost friend woke up a little bit earlier than anticipated. Long time no see, Georgina."

His presence surprised her and was evident to him immediately.

"Oh, now, don't be rude, Georgina. Is this a way to welcome your old business partner?"

"We were never business partners, Gustav."

He made three clicking noises with his tongue against his teeth expressing his annoyance over her insult then took a seat in one of the wingback chairs opposite her. Dressed in a designer tuxedo he looked every bit the suave, sophisticated man she remembered.

"Well, be that as it may, by my account we were until, of course, you decided to blow the whistle on me and rat me out, that is. I must confess, I never saw that coming. And here we are. Two decades later, a little reunion is what this is. Wouldn't you agree?"

She didn't give him the satisfaction of answering his question, fighting hard to suppress the anger that slowly rose into her chest.

"What's the matter, Georgina? Cat got your tongue all of a sudden? Well, let's see if we can do something about that, shall we?"

She didn't like the mocking warning that sat behind his eyes. Something told her he was up to something and she was not going to like it.

He got up and took a tobacco pipe from a gold box on the mantelpiece, filling it and then lighting it up, puffing big balls of cherry fragranced smoke into the air. Next, he took his time heating one of the pokers between the blazing flames in the fireplace.

"What were you doing at the bank?"

There was a steely edge to his question.

"Getting lunch money."

He inspected the glowing fire poker.

"It's going to be like that then, is it? You know, Georgina, you are not giving me enough credit. You still think you are smarter than me. Did you honestly think you could waltz back into my city undetected? You forget that we created this disguise of yours together."

She smiled, intentionally hinting that she might have planned it that way.

"Ah, and there it is again, the bit where you think you are smarter than me. I see right through you, Georgina. You knew I'd track you down looking like that and, in the event that I captured you, I'd bring you to my house, one you'd escape from easily because you consulted on the security system."

She tried not to reveal that he had guessed her plan to a tee, so she looked blankly at his face.

"But here's the thing, dear friend, I learned a thing or two in that prison you had me locked away in. I met a few, shall we say, business consultants who taught me a thing or two. Not to mention that I had a lot of time to think. And here we are, tucked away in my lake house instead where I had a very impressive security system installed that I am positive not even you can escape from."

In the furthest corner of the room, a cuckoo clock sounded the time and he turned to take note of the time. Looking annoyed, he placed the poker back in its stand.

"I guess we will have to continue this conversation a little later. I have more pressing guests to attend to." He smoothed his already perfectly groomed hair with his comb then pivoted and left the room.

CHAPTER TWENTY-EIGHT

When she was certain Gustav had left the room, knowing where he was headed, Jorja attempted to free her hands once more. But, as with the first attempt, the ropes didn't budge and she resorted to jumping the chair toward the fire poker set. The chair's feet caught on the carpet and planted her face-first into the Persian rug. It nearly knocked her breath out but she soon recovered and wriggled her body like a snake attached to its prey toward the companion set. Out of breath and making hardly any progress at all, she paused when she heard footsteps approaching.

Her heart pounded noisily in her temples as she listened, praying Gustav had not decided to return. She tried twisting her body toward the door, to see better, but her angle was off.

The footsteps grew louder and her heart beat loudly in

her chest, stopped in place only by the fear that wedged in her throat. She searched anxiously for another way out, wriggling her body faster toward the poker, grasping at any opportunity to save herself. Suddenly the footsteps were in the room with her, rapidly moving toward her, stopping right behind her.

Out of her line of sight, the smooth clanking sound of a switchblade springing from its shaft was unmistakable; telling her the owner of the footsteps was there to kill her.

She pinched her eyes shut, tried to ready herself for the stabbing. A strong hand held her arms in place.

This time, there was no way out.

Overcome by emotion, her life flashing before her, she shot up a prayer to the only one left to rescue her. It didn't matter if God heard her or not, or even if she fully believed that he would. All that mattered was that she at least gave it a last shot.

But unexpectedly, her miracle didn't come in the way she had imagined and moments later Ben's deep assuring voice whispered close to her ear.

"See what happens when you start the party without me?"

The knife freed her hands and she pushed herself upright. When her eyes confirmed that she wasn't imagining it, she could no longer hold back her emotions.

"Ben! How did you—?"

"The oldest trick in the book, my dear. I planted a tracker on your jacket. Of course, the rest was left to my accomplished skill set when you left the jacket at the hotel, but, hey, not the time to get into that now."

His strong arms helped her to her feet and she threw her arms around him.

"You're welcome. Now let's get out of here."

But once again, Jorja was faced with a decision. Choosing the tugging she so strongly felt was from God, or choose the path she had obsessed over for all of two decades. And as her mind once more clouded her spirit, she reasoned that she was not in God's way, but that God was in her way, and that perhaps, if he was as gracious as they said he was, he would wait for her, just a little longer.

"I can't, not yet."

"What? Why not?"

"I have to finish what I started twenty years ago. I have to put Gustav Züber behind bars for the rest of his life. This time, for good."

"You're insane, Georgina, let's get out of here. Let sleeping dogs lie. People like that eventually hang themselves. We have a chance to start over, enjoy what's left of our lives together, finally, just like we were meant to do a long time ago."

Ben's piercing blue eyes were holding her hostage and every cell inside her body wanted to give in to his—and God's—plea, but she couldn't, not yet. She couldn't let Gustav get away with what he had done to Ewan, to her, to her life. So strong was the anger that had been buried inside her for so long that she couldn't think clearly anymore. Like a festering sore, that had suddenly erupted to the surface, all she knew was that he needed to pay and that she was the only one who could make it happen.

From somewhere outside the house they heard movement, distant voices, footsteps on the deck outside.

"We're out of time, Georgina! The alarm must have overridden my transmitter. If we don't get out of here right now we're dead!"

But Jorja was already on the move, darting to the wide stone staircase that led upstairs.

"Georgina! What are you doing? They're already at the door."

"I need to find a computer. I need to send these files right now," she whisper-shouted back, already halfway up the stairs.

"Now? I have one back at the B&B, let's go!"

"He murdered my friend, Ben, used me back then, robbed me of my entire future! He cannot get away with it. Not again."

She was already upstairs in Gustav's office, bounding toward the computer on his desk.

"Yes, and he won't. But it will not do us any good if he catches us before you get a chance to do it. Then all this was for nothing."

But vengeance blinded her judgment and Jorja was already on the computer attempting to crack the access password.

In the sitting room below them, Gustav's voice echoed up the stairs as he shouted commands at his men.

"She's in the house somewhere. Find her!"

Ben leaned in over her shoulder and once more urged her to come to her senses.

"He's coming for us, Georgina. It's not too late. We can escape over the balcony. Please! He almost killed you before, and he will not hesitate to do so the second he walks up those stairs and sees you. Georgina, vengeance is not as sweet as you might think it is. You will not be free, ever. Even if you do succeed right now, and Züber goes to jail for the rest of his life, he will leave no stone unturned until he hunts you down again, even from behind bars."

Her hand reached inside her blouse and she took out the flash drive.

"It will be quick," she assured him holding the memory stick up to his face.

Urgent footsteps on the stairs rushed toward them. And with not a second to spare, Ben's eyes apologized as he snatched the memory stick from her hand and yanked her toward the balcony door. She fought back.

"I need to do this, Ben, please? It's the only way. He can't get away with it!"

She wrestled the flash drive from his grip and shot back to the computer, inserting it into the dock to complete her mission.

"You're blinded by revenge, Jorja, and it's going to get us both killed today."

But she didn't care. Nothing Ben said could persuade her to stop. Her mind and emotions were no longer under her control like a volcano that had lain dormant for two decades needing to burst through the hard crusty layers that kept it contained.

Her fingers moved quickly on the keys while Ben had already opened the balcony doors to prepare for any final opportunity to escape. Alert, he stood guard, ready to fend off the imminent threat rushing toward them, trapped in a web of loyalty and love.

But as Jorja pressed the key that finally launched the data on the drive into cyberspace, time had run out along with it.

Two men exploded through the doors of Gustav's office, shotguns aimed at their heads crushing any chance they might have had to escape over the balcony. Held hostage by their guns, there was now no way out.

Jorja glanced sideways at the blinking red light on the drive, and the laptop in front of her telling her the files were not done sending. Behind her, Ben's heart pounded wildly in his chest, his mind fighting for a way out. Their hands were in the air, but the guards took aim to shoot if they as much as moved an inch, pausing as they waited for Gustav to arrive to give the instruction.

Desperate to divert their attention away from the computer, Jorja stepped closer to the balcony, risking whatever she needed to save her cause—even Ben.

Her movement instantly had the guards on edge, their

bodies rigid in their stance to shoot, their voices intimidating when they warned her to stop.

"Don't move!" one yelled as he lunged his gun toward them.

She watched his fingers tense over the trigger, his veins expand in his thick neck, knew that he was not bluffing.

To her left, the light on the drive remained red. Dying was not an option, not yet. Not without seeing Gustav Züber squirm when he realized she had taken from him what he had taken from her.

CHAPTER TWENTY-NINE

"Well, will you look at this?" Gustav's voice cut through the silence as he walked into the room, ordering his guards to ease off and allow him to speak first.

As they flanked him, his eyes flickered with smugness and arrogance. He had won. And though it taunted her to see him relishing in his victory, Jorja suppressed the urge to tell him what she thought of him. His day of reckoning was upon him. Victory would be hers soon. She would wait it out, and when it finally came, it would be every bit as sweet as she expected it to be. For now, his presence provided her with the much-needed time the computer disk required to complete sending the files. So she would let him mock her with his eyes, bite her lip, hold her cards close to her chest, knowing that he wouldn't be smiling for long.

Their eyes locked, his intensely staring into hers, like bulls preparing to fight. Then Gustav finally spoke again.

"I always knew you weren't acting alone. I mean you were good, make no mistake, the best if I am truthful. But I always knew there was no way you could have cracked some of those security systems on your own. I just didn't care to know back then. As long as you got me what I needed I was content. But here I am. Finally meeting the man who most probably helped you put me behind bars. Not necessarily the introduction I would have liked, but I am not going to pass up the opportunity to meet the man behind the world's once master art thief, caught like a deer in a trap right here in my own house. And under duress, I might add! It's a dream come true if you ask me."

Gustav's voice was mocking but under the sarcastic tone and flattering words, it oddly hinted at admiration, but something else laced his tone. As if he knew something she didn't. Something she couldn't quite put her finger on yet. Trapped by their enemy and two armed men, Ben and Jorja stood side-by-side and faced their imminent fate. But now that he had said what he needed to, Jorja couldn't ignore that time was no longer on their side. Careful not to alert Gustav, she sneaked another glance at the drive. The light had turned green. It was finally over. She had succeeded in exposing every clandestine transaction this man had ever made. Thanks to her, his entire business was now in jeopardy and, even if he one day did get out of prison again, he would have nothing to come home to this time. The contents of the flash drive had burned every bridge he had ever built to the ground and there was no way back from it.

But knowing what was to come his way would have to be enough. If she did not make it out of here alive to see his face when it happened, she would be okay with it.

Her eyes searched the corners of the room for a way out, evoking Gustav to react with laughter.

"Oh, that's priceless, you're already looking for an escape. Let me save you the trouble, Georgina. There is a reason I chose to keep you here in this little hidden gem of mine in the first place. I have made some, how shall I put this, associations during my time spent behind bars. Associations that are light years ahead of you and your old pal here. Not to mention that I do still have a lot of confidants of my own in high places, very high places. Friends who owe me favors, some of which I was forced to call upon earlier than I had anticipated when you turned on me. Nonetheless, it allowed me to make a few modifications to my once antiquated security system. I think you might be quite impressed by it. You will find the security in my house now tighter than that of the Bank of Spain's, and not even you can break in or out of this place. Take them!" He shifted gears and commanded his men to take Ben and Jorja captive. He had made his little celebratory speech.

And she didn't care anymore if he killed her. She had done what she needed to do. But Ben, she could not let his death be on her conscience too.

"Let Ben go, Gustav. He has nothing to do with this. This is between you and me." She made a desperate plea.

Intrigued, Züber told his men to wait as he stepped toward his prisoners.

"And why would I do that, huh? I reckon the two of you might come in very handy in my future endeavors. Like I said, Georgina, we are partners, always have been, always will be. The way I see it, you owe me. Without me, you would have never had the opportunity to create the illustrious title you are now so desperately clinging to. You are no good to me dead. But as long as I have the upper hand, you, and your skilled friend, will do exactly as I say."

He snapped his fingers to have his men take hold of Ben and Jorja, then turned his back on them as he walked toward the door, and lay all his cards on the table when he stopped to say,

"Time is often a luxury most businessmen don't have. But when the world suddenly hands you nothing but time on a silver platter, it affords people like me the very commodity that is the most valuable of all in our line of business. Time to plan our next heist. I already told you. You are worth more to me alive than dead. Now, if you will excuse me, I am late for my banquet. Can't leave my esteemed guests waiting. Who knows what profits are to be made?" He smiled then barked a command at his men.

"Tie them up. I'll deal with them later. And this time, do a proper job of it."

· · ·

GUSTAV'S REVELATION burned in their minds as the armed men took them captive. He had not planned to kill them after all. He needed them, both of them. Though relieved to hear their lives would be spared for his selfish gains, she could not deny that the prospect of getting back into the business was exciting. Even if under Gustav's coercion. And she knew deep down inside Ben felt the same and that he would leap at the chance too.

The armed men took them downstairs to the sitting room where they tied them to chairs in the middle of the room. When they left, they took the fire pokers with them as if they knew this was what she had planned the first time she tried to escape. Of course, she thought as her eyes found the cameras in the corners of the room. They were watching. That's how they knew Ben had come for her.

After the men left them alone in the room and disappeared through a door they locked behind them, Ben spoke for the first time.

"I'm not going to say I told you so." His voice was calm and steady, his tone almost melancholy.

"Good, then don't," she replied, as she watched him wriggle in an attempt to loosen the far too tight ropes around his body.

"No, you know what? I am going to say it. I told you so! This is exactly what I said would happen. Now we're stuck here with no way out and the tantalizing prospect of being forced into pulling heists for this evil man again."

"And what's so bad about that, Ben? Are you telling me the idea doesn't excite you?"

He stopped to look at her.

"Are you hearing yourself? None of this would have happened if you had listened to me. Georgina, you know how I feel about you, but you are so blinded by your vendetta to get back at Gustav that you have lost all logic. We cannot go back to pulling art heists. It's insane! We've been out of it for two decades. Everything has changed. We have changed. You might have been at the top of your game back then but that was a long time ago. I am not ready to die, Georgina. We were kids back then. And spending the rest of the days the good Lord grants me behind bars isn't how I'd like to spend my retirement either."

Ben's voice had turned gentle and warm, like his eyes. He was right; her heart had been consumed with hatred and malice. But that was not the part that had suddenly taken her by surprise, caught her emotions in her throat. Including God in his plea for her to let it go, reminded her of the person she had become and the life she lived in St. Ives.

And that person was not filled with anger and vengeful thoughts. Looking into Ben's eyes she realized she had lost focus, forgotten whom Ewan fought so hard for. Tears welled in her eyes as she recalled his parting words. *Leave anger to God.*

As her heart and mind pondered the last words her

friend spoke to her, it was as if a flash of lightning shocked her into understanding. At the time she did not know why he had said it, or even what it meant, but right now, staring into the eyes of the man she loved more than anyone else in the world, she knew what Ewan had tried to tell her. His words were meant to warn her, as if he knew precisely what was to come. Once again, he was protecting her, warning her to be careful, telling her not to let vengeance rule her heart.

And at that moment, as her heart filled with sadness, and tears flooded her eyes, she also understood why Ewan had given her the fridge magnet. Because ever since he had met her, Ewan had tried to help her, like an angel placed beside her, guiding and protecting her. He had seen the wall she had built around her, to protect herself—to shut him out, and to stop God from coming in. All Ewan had ever wanted for her was peace, God's peace. And peace did not come from seeking vengeance on the ones who'd harmed her.

Jorja's shoulders shook beneath the ropes as she recalled the words on her refrigerator.

The Lord is my shepherd, I shall not be in want.
He makes me lie down in green pastures,
He leads me beside quiet waters,
He restores my soul.

And as the words looped in her mind and heart, she

asked God to forgive her, to restore her soul, to lead her beside quiet waters.

When she had confessed her heart to God, she turned her watery gaze to Ben and asked that he forgave her too. And as God released his grace on her and set her free, she said, "Georgina no longer exists. My name is Jorja."

As her words echoed in the sanctified space between them, the sound of gunshots outside the house warned them that their past was still very much present and that it was far from over.

CHAPTER THIRTY

The gunfire grew louder, pounding against the doors and walls of the house outside. Bullets smashed through the windows, scattering glass in every direction.

Ben flinched as the bullets whistled past them and penetrated the walls next to them.

"Get down!" He yelled for Jorja to overturn her chair.

The two armed men exploded from their room and lunged toward the door behind Jorja and Ben, releasing rapid fire in retaliation against the unseen enemy.

"Hey! Untie us!" Jorja yelled after them, but her words were spoken in vain when first one captor, then the other collapsed dead onto the floor.

"We need to find a way out of here, Jorja!" Ben shouted as more bullets rained onto the house.

Their bodies strained against the ropes, desperate to

break free. Glass and splintered pieces of wood and fabric exploded all around them as if the devil had unleashed his demons in a ruthless attack on all who no longer worshipped him. Jorja prayed that God protected them, prayed that she would get the chance to get to know him better, prayed for a way out.

At the far end of the room, a loud crashing noise erupted into flames that danced on the floor behind them. The attackers had thrown a firebomb through the window, which exploded the moment it hit the floor. Almost instantly, it climbed the heavy drapes and set the room on fire. Smoke filled their lungs as Jorja and Ben wrestled to untie each other's hands—they had managed to turn their chairs' backs toward each other.

"It's too tight!" Jorja announced when her fingers could not untie Ben's ropes.

Their eyes searched the smoke-filled room for any pieces of glass nearby, but all they found were shards too small to cut through the ropes.

Through the thick black smoke that threatened to unleash its power upon them, Gustav's face suddenly appeared.

Angst gripped Jorja as she spotted him first. In his hand, a large carving knife came toward them.

"Watch out!" she warned Ben, simultaneously attempting to turn herself around to kick Gustav in the shin.

But he was already on top of them, driving the knife in

their direction. The blade sliced through the fibered strands, instantly setting them both free.

"Follow me!" he yelled and hastily moved toward the only wall on the far end of an adjacent room that the flames had not yet reached. Now visible only by the soft folds in the wallpaper, a hidden alcove revealed an elevator behind it and he hurried them inside.

Left with no other way of escaping the unceasing attack on them, they complied and followed him inside.

"Not that I am ungrateful to you for saving our lives but care to tell us what on earth is going on out there?" Ben demanded answers as the elevator started its descent.

"It's Artem Sokolov. We walked straight into an ambush. My entire property is crawling with his men."

"Where are you taking us?" Jorja asked.

"I told you, I'm not done with you yet. I need you and you are no good to me dead."

"You should have left us to die, Gustav. I don't know what you are planning but we don't want any part of it. We are done pulling jobs for you or anyone else." Jorja's voice was surprisingly calm, her words cut short when the doors opened to an underground tunnel.

"Trust me, Georgina, once you hear what we're after you are going to have a hard time standing up to your seemingly unwavering resolve, I assure you."

"No, I won't, and my name isn't Georgina anymore, it's Jorja."

"You don't need to tell me that *Ms. Rose*." He emphasized her last name, intentionally letting her know that he already knew the information she'd just shared. "Now stop doubting my good intentions and get moving before they discover our escape route."

"What is this anyway?" Ben asked, taking in the narrow underground tunnel's amber stone walls.

"It's your one ticket to freedom, that's what this is, but don't fear, you are perfectly safe down here. These tunnels have withstood time for over a century," Gustav said.

"We're not. We just don't want to be in the same confined space as you. Like I said, we're not interested," Jorja replied.

Gustav stopped dead to turn and face her, his intense eyes doing what he did so well; lure people into his deceitful ways.

"You will, and you want to know why I am so sure of it? Because you have never been able to back away from a challenge, especially one said to be impossible."

Jorja's heart skipped several beats, once again taunted by the prospect of returning to what she'd once lived and breathed.

"Give it up, Jorja. It's written all over your face, in glorious artful strokes. Admit it. You miss the thrill. That exhilarating rush you get when breaking in, the challenge of the escape, the money. You want this as much as I do. Stop fighting it." Gustav's penetrating gaze probed her, luring her into confessing what she knew deep down was the truth.

"You heard her, Züber, now give it a rest," Ben said to break the spell he'd cast on her.

But Gustav Züber was a man who always got his way and in the confines of the underground getaway tunnel, took a few steps back and drew on the only thing he had left in his arsenal of tricks to strong-arm them. When he aimed the small pearl-grip revolver at them, his voice was cold and threatening.

"As I said, you will, one way or another. Now walk!"

He ushered them to move in front of him, poking the gun in their backs in turn to propel them forward.

"What could possibly be so important to you that you need us for it, huh? I am sure you have acquainted yourself with plenty of lowlife scum like you who would be more than willing to do your dirty work for you, " Jorja spat back.

Gustav let out a victorious squeal.

"See, I told you! You cannot resist, Georgina, Jorja, or whoever you think you need to be. We were born to do this, it's in our blood, pumping, surging through every cell in our bodies. I already have a buyer lined up for it too, and it's a big fish. The biggest you have ever seen. It will be the last job we ever need to do. Putting me behind bars was the biggest mistake you could ever make. It cost me valuable time in securing my retirement resources, Jorja, and you are solely to blame for it. So now, you have to earn your freedom, and that freedom comes at a hefty price. Such a hefty price that it can only be ransomed against one exquisite piece of art. I want Da Vinci's *Salvator Mundi*.

And you two are going to get it for me, willingly or not, your choice. Now walk!"

He shoved the gun between her shoulder blades, thrusting her forward. She winced at the agony it shot through her bad arm that was now throbbing painfully after the events of the past few hours.

"Hey, take it easy!" Ben yelled.

"Then shut your mouths and keep walking."

"It's impossible to get the painting, Gustav, and you know it." Jorja pulled the conversation back to the heist, desperate to talk their way out of the task he was forcing upon them.

"Well, isn't that why I've got you?"

"Not even I can find it. That piece disappeared off the face of the earth a long time ago, and you know it. The entire world has been looking for it and no one's been able to pick up even the slightest trace.

"Au contraire, my dear. I told you. Prison might have kept me in one place but I didn't let that stop me. I have already found the trail of breadcrumbs it has left behind, done the heavy lifting for you. All you have to do is exert your special skills and bring it home to me. And since you have your sidekick to hand, well, I guess it will be even easier than I had planned. And wait until you find out where the painting is. Go on, take a guess," he nudged her excitedly when she didn't bite.

"I'm not going to play this silly game of yours to feed your narcissistic ego, Gustav."

"Fine, killjoy, I'll give in and tell you. It's in one of the world's most sprawling metropolises. Abu Dhabi." His voice was drenched in exhilaration and teasing with adventure.

"Well, good luck with that, mate." Ben spoiled his fun.

"No one asked you, sidekick. I am guessing you will do anything Jorja asks you anyway, so shut it and walk. We're almost there."

"And where might that be exactly? It's a dead end up ahead." Jorja had already spotted the wall at the end of the narrow tunnel.

"Patience is a virtue, my dear. Have you already forgotten that vital skill? You had best be dusting off your toolkit. I'm not having you mess this up for me. Age isn't on my side anymore, another thing I have you to thank for."

She didn't give him the satisfaction of challenging him any further. She understood patience all too well. His days were numbered. By the time the sun came up, McGuthrey would find the biggest story of his small-town career right there on his computer when he switched it on. Knowing him, he would be taking it straight to the *Daily Mail* before teatime came round and it would be game over for Gustav Züber, forever.

She stood aside to see Gustav reveal a retina scanner behind an imitation stone in the wall. When the scan detected the programmed match, the concealed door sprang open.

"After you," he insisted, waggling his gun for them to

get into another elevator before he stepped inside next to them.

As the elevator ascended, he made a final plea to win Jorja's cooperation in his plot.

"Get me the Da Vinci and I promise you will never hear from me again."

"Not going to happen, Gustav. I'm not the same person I was back then and I'm not going back to that life either. Like I said earlier, you should have saved yourself the trouble of rescuing us. Our paths diverge here."

His guard was down and she thought of plowing him to the ground, but her body was not up to it—she had been through too much over the past few days to withstand another blow to her body. She had said what she needed to and knew what was to come.

The elevator doors opened before he could answer and he stepped out into another house every bit as homely as the one they had just left behind.

But it seemed they had all underestimated one of their biggest threats as they set eyes upon five men who instantly pushed them to the ground.

Caught entirely off guard by the surprise attack that awaited them, the men held them down, pinning their bodies to the floor. Jorja wrestled as much as her injured body would allow, Ben too, but their attempt to ward off the ambush proved futile as they instantly felt sharp needles pierce the soft flesh on the side of their necks.

Moments later the room spun in unsteady circles around them before everything went black.

CHAPTER 31

Jorja's feet dangled beneath her limp body as her mind slowly came back to life. Apart from the dull ache pounding against her brow, she felt little else.

She tried raising her head but was barely able to move. It felt leaden and unresponsive. The fluid that had formed in the center of her bottom lip threatened to drop onto the floor and told her that she was suspended, not lying down.

Turning her attention to the senses she had left, she heard nothing but silence at first. But, as her perception became more vivid, she was certain she was not alone. Movement caught her attention to her right and she tried turning her head sideways to listen. There was shallow breathing, right beside her. Her mind instantly went to Ben and she tried calling out his name. But the poison hadn't worn off yet and it had left her tongue thick and bitter tasting. The vile sensation in her mouth made her feel sick and she fought back the urge to throw up. Desperate to make sense of it all she willed her mind into consciousness and soon fragments of memories cut through the blanket of fog that held her mind captive.

She recalled the sharp sting in her neck, Gustav's frantic shouting next to her, and Ben's strong hand in hers. They'd been ambushed, taken by surprise, and driven to the ground without so much as a chance to fight off Sokolov's men. Then sobering thoughts drove through the fog. They were still alive, at least she was.

"Ben," she forced his name from her numb lips, then listened.

Next to her, she heard him moan, barely audible, but she was certain it was him. She shot up a prayer of thanks that he was still alive and again called out to him. This time his voice was louder. Still unable to lift her head much she forced her heavy eyelids open. Her vision was blurry but she soon traced the outlines of his body next to her. Like her, he was suspended from the roof; his hands bound high above his head.

Desperate to gain control of her body again, she tried moving her feet beneath her to support her weight. It worked but her body weighed a ton and her injured arm suddenly shot immeasurable pain through her shoulder. They had tied her hands above her head too, unaware of the injury to her arm. Suddenly emotions overtook her and she tried to fight back the urge to cry but couldn't. Tears streamed down her cheeks. They were tears of gratitude for being alive, but mostly tears of fear for what was yet unknown. Sokolov could have easily killed them, yet he hadn't. Why? And where was Gustav?

With her sight now almost fully restored and the nerve-endings in her body slowly coming to life, she managed to lift her head off her chest. Next to her Ben moaned as his body also steadily came alive.

"Ben, can you hear me?"

He moaned a response.

"You're okay, it's just the effects of the toxin still wearing off. Give it a few minutes."

The feeling in her legs had slowly returned and she managed to put her full body weight on her legs to stand. The motion instantly released the tension of the chains on her hands and arms.

Glimpses of clay-colored cobbles eventually flowed into a powdery amber floor. At first thought, it felt similar to that of a dank cellar of sorts, but it was far too expansive. There was something eerie about it, like death was present.

Gustav was nowhere to be seen and she looked over her shoulder searching for him. Loose chains similar to the ones that bound her and Ben were dangling slightly behind her and to her left. Fear suddenly gripped her. What if they had already killed him and they were coming for her or Ben next? She trembled at the thought of being tortured first. Sokolov had every reason to hold a grudge against her, and certainly against Gustav.

Ben's voice had her turn to face him.

"Jorja, did they hurt you?"

"No, I'm fine. You?" She noticed a deep cut above his nose and the dried blood on his skin.

"I'll live."

On his feet now too, he yanked at the chain above his head.

"It's no use. Save your energy."

She saw Ben searching the space.

"I think we're underground somewhere, maybe a cellar," she announced.

"Or a dungeon," Ben cut in.

"They took Gustav, at least, I think they did. Look." She pushed her head back over her left shoulder to point out the shackles that dangled from the chain.

"What if Sokolov tortured him to give back his money?"

"Then he got what he deserved."

"No one deserves death, Ben, no matter how much we despise him."

She bit down on her lip, forcing herself not to ask if he thought they'd come for her next. But Ben had sensed her burning question already.

"If he wanted us dead, his men would have killed us already."

She was about to offer her thoughts when the sound of keys clanked against a door somewhere in front of them. They listened as an iron bolt scraped against metal before the door creaked open.

Feet shuffled toward them. As the faint light brought them into vision Jorja saw two burly men dragging Gustav toward them. When they were close enough and his face came into view she saw he had been beaten. Her body tensed, steeling herself for what might be her fate next.

"What did you do to him? Why are we here?" she dared to ask.

The men ignored her questions and finished securing Züber to the chains. When they were done they moved to one side, hands clasped in front of them like military men waiting for their next command.

Once more, footsteps announced the arrival of another captor and they pinned their eyes onto the shadowy outlines of a well-dressed man as he slowly moved into the light in front of them.

Jorja recognized him the instant the light fell on his deep-set eyes that peered at her from beneath his heavy black brows. Artem Sokolov's angry gaze sliced into her soul, making her heart plunge to her stomach with dread.

She wanted to say something but her tongue caught in her throat and she tore her eyes away from his intense gaze instead.

He moved closer, so close that she could smell his expensive cologne, taste the vodka on his breath when he spoke.

"Your business partner is refusing to cooperate with me, Ms. Rose, so I am wondering what to do next."

"He's not my business partner," she replied, her tone icy.

Sokolov's eyes narrowed.

"I don't like liars, Jorja, especially if they lie to my face."

"She's not lying," Ben jumped to her defense.

"Tell your boyfriend to shut his mouth."

He let his unspoken threat linger before he spoke again.

"Do you know why I had my men bring you here instead of killing you?"

She refused to answer.

"Fine, I will tell you. You and Mr. Züber cost me millions, not to mention the damage caused to my family name. So I thought to myself, I could turn a blind eye and let my men have the satisfaction of killing you, or I can do it myself. Naturally, you can understand that it will bring me much more pleasure to see you beg for your life before I kill you, right? So here we are."

He turned to one of his men who handed him a gun before taking up his position again.

"But here is my problem. I don't know which one of you to kill first." He let out a sadistic laugh that echoed through the underground space.

Resting the tip of the gun against his dimpled chin he looked at Gustav who was barely conscious.

"Mr. Züber was my first choice because, well, it's obvious he ran the show and should therefore die first. But then I didn't expect to be lucky enough to also have your boyfriend join us."

"Leave him out of this, Sokolov. He had nothing to do with what happened," Jorja begged.

He laughed again.

"That is precisely my problem, Jorja. You see, to derive maximum satisfaction from this vengeful situation, killing him first will undoubtedly hurt you most. See where I'm going with this?"

His phone buzzed in his pocket and he stopped to read the text. Anger instantly flushed his cheeks as he read it and seconds later dropped the phone back into his pocket. He took a few steps back then aimed his gun at Ben.

"Decision made, he goes first, then you, and finally Züber. Not only did the two of you steal from me, but now Züber's entire double-dealing business and client list is in every newspaper across the globe! Losing money is one thing, but taking my children's inheritance and tarnishing my family name is an entirely different situation!"

He aimed the gun at Ben's chest, then turned to see the pain that Ben's death would render in Jorja's eyes.

"No wait!" she yelled.

"Let us go and I will not only get all your money back, but I will clear your name and ensure you have enough bargaining power to keep you out of jail for a very long time."

Sokolov's gaze probed her face but he held his aim, so Jorja tried to negotiate with him once more.

"I can get you the *Salvator Mundi*."

THANK you for reading VENGEANCE IS MINE! I hope you loved Jorja Rose as much as I do.

Jorja's perilous journey continues in **book 2, SHADOW OF FEAR.**

Will she be able to make true on her bargain with Sokolov or did she promise more than she can handle? One-click Shadow of Fear now!

"Urcelia has outdone herself. Fast pace...who can Jorja trust when she's not sure if she can trust herself, or God. Will she be able to save Ben and will Jorja find her faith in God? If you liked Vengeance is Mine you will double love Shadow of Fear."

BOOK 2:

Enemies collide in the second installment of the toe-curling Christian Suspense Thriller that left readers gasping for more at the end of book one!

What seemed like the end was really the beginning.

Retaliation blinds Jorja as she hunts down her enemies, hoping to put her past behind her for good.

Only to find that breaking free isn't as easy as she thought it would be. Blood was shed, lives were lost, and now more lives are at stake. Caught in a deadlock between enemies who won't stop until they serve revenge, Jorja has to make a choice.

Make a deal with the devil, or die!

Her choice sets in motion one of the biggest assignments she has ever undertaken. One where fear threatens to seize her heart and take her soul.

Can she finally break free from death's clutches and risk it all one more time?

Read and find out!

I appreciate your help in spreading the word, including telling a friend. Reviews help readers find books! Please leave a review on your favorite book site.

You can also visit my online store (https://shop.urcelia.-com) for exclusive deals, merchandise, and discounted book bundles.

Turn the page for an excerpt from SHADOW OF FEAR.

EXCERPT FROM SHADOW OF FEAR - BOOK II

SHADOW OF FEAR

(Book 2 in this series)

CHAPTER ONE

Silence fell as Jorja's words left her mouth and held Artem Sokolov's attention hostage. His dark eyes pierced her soul, searching, intruding, verifying her pledge.

"I can get you the *Salvator Mundi*," she repeated again, her voice slightly desperate as her eyes darted back and forth between Ben and the gun in Sokolov's hand.

"I heard you, Jorja. I just don't believe you." Sokolov called her bluff.

"It's the truth. I will get it for you if you let us go—all of us."

Something in Sokolov's eyes revealed that she had piqued his curiosity. She'd successfully hooked him, bought them some time.

But he wasn't budging.

Her heart pounded in her chest, her mind frantically searching for what to say next that would clinch the deal toward their freedom.

"It's worth a lot of money, Artem. Half a million dollars by the most recent estimate, but it's worth a lot more to you in collateral."

She kept his gaze and waited for him to respond. Except he didn't. Instead, Gustav spoke.

"You're a traitor, Georgina." Gustav's strained voice rang in her ears as he spat a ball of bloodied saliva towards her. Sokolov laughed aloud at Gustav's unintentional confession before lowering the gun next to his side. "See, I knew you were hiding something, Züber. The two of you were planning a heist after all. And you said you weren't partners anymore." His tongue clicked against his teeth in disapproval as he moved to stand in front of Jorja.

"You surprise me, Jorja. I must confess. You had me for a moment. But that's what you are good at, isn't it? Being the mistress of deceit."

"We weren't planning anything, Artem. I didn't lie to you."

"She's a liar!" Gustav yelled out. "Everything she says is a lie."

His outburst had no effect on Sokolov, whose gaze

continued to stare Jorja down. His eyes told her that he didn't believe her and as his hand lifted away from his side once more to point his gun at Ben's face, his cellphone rang.

The ringtone was that of a merry-go-round's and it instantly snapped Sokolov's attention away from them. He dropped his aim and turned to take the call. When, a few moments later, his face revealed that the call must have been from one of his children, Jorja silently prayed it would have him leave the room. She needed more time to solidify her plan, to find out what Gustav knew.

When Sokolov ended the call, he handed his gun to one of his henchmen before facing his captives. Once more, his eyes were on Jorja.

"You must think me a fool, Jorja. The *Salvator Mundi* was purchased in a legal auction several years ago and I happen to know who bought it. I don't steal from my friends, not even to save my own skin."

He turned and swiftly left the room, his men following close behind him.

When the door closed behind Sokolov and his three prisoners were left alone, Gustav wasted no time.

"I should've known better than to get in bed with the likes of you again. You're an idiot, Georgina. You think you can bargain your way out of this, but you're dead wrong. Artem Sokolov will kill us the moment you hand over that painting."

"If you have a better idea to get us out of this mess

alive, Gustav, then by all means, spit it out. I did what any normal human would do when a gun is pointed at her face."

"Yes, well, I guess it blew up in your face, didn't it? He'll be back and then he will finish us all off."

Jorja paused and ignored his bitter tirade. Her instincts were suddenly alive and she knew exactly why. "You don't know where it is, do you."

Gustav's expression revealed she had successfully guessed the truth.

"How did I not see that? You are the fraud you've always been, Gustav Züber! You don't have any idea where that painting is. Sokolov was right. It was sold via proxy at an auction and to this day, no one knows for certain who bought it or where it is. It's been missing for years. I cannot believe I fell for it."

Jorja looked away. Her insides were alive with fury. More than that, her body felt numb with fear.

She looked apologetically at Ben, whose warm eyes told her that everything would be okay. But she knew it wouldn't. She had made a promise she could not deliver on. A promise made in good faith trusting a sworn enemy who had nothing but malice toward her. They were going to die, all of them, down in the dungeons where their murders would be hidden from the world, their identities dissolved as if they'd never existed.

Near silent sobs pushed into her throat as she hung helplessly from the rafters above.

"You played me, Gustav. Our death will be on your head. This is all on you. You'll as much as pull the trigger yourself when he kills us. But the joke is on you, Gustav. During all our times together, you'd always told me how you wanted the world to remember you. The great Gustav Züber. Art extraordinaire. Master appraiser. But you are nothing more than a lowly murderer, a liar. That's the legacy you'll be leaving behind. That's how the world will remember you. A cheating murderer." Her voice sounded dejected.

"I didn't play you, Georgina, and I'm not a murderer! I told you. I made many friends in prison and it just so happens that one of them is a member of a French mob. He told me the painting was hidden behind a wall somewhere in Abu Dhabi, and that he knew where."

"And let me guess. You promised him a cut when I stole it for you, didn't you?"

"Five percent. That's it. The rest is ours."

"Are you listening to yourself, Züber?" Ben spoke for the first time since Sokolov left. "You're talking as if there is still a deal on the table, trusting our lives in the hands of a French mobster's tip-off. That's if this mobster friend of yours is, in fact, even telling you the truth. Because, if he really knew where it was, then why not just steal it himself? You were duped, man, and now we're all going to die because of it."

"I wasn't *duped*. He had it on good authority. I trust him."

"Trust him? You're insane, Züber. The man's a gangster who will say anything you want to hear when you share a jail cell," Ben scoffed.

"It doesn't matter now anyway," Jorja said. "Who cares if your French mobster friend told the truth or not. Sokolov has one up on us. Criminals like him are all in cahoots with one another. Heck, it might even be hidden behind one of his walls for all we know."

"The man told me the truth. Once you share a cell with an inmate there's a bond nothing can break. We stood together, had each other's backs. He's good for it."

"Like I said, Gustav, it doesn't matter. Sokolov isn't interested. We don't have any bargaining power without a worthwhile trade," Jorja reasoned.

"Oh, Artem Sokolov will come around. Just you wait and see. I've done enough business with him over the years to know what it looks like when a man has his back against the wall. You were right about one thing, Jorja. The *Salvator Mundi* was auctioned and bought by proxy, but it left the auction house and never made it to its destination. You, of all people, should know the bounty that would have been placed on that painting. I can think of at least a dozen very influential men who would have paid a small fortune to intercept that transfer. And as it happens, my guy worked for one of them."

Their conversation was interrupted when Sokolov re-entered the room. His facial expression looked noticeably different from when he had left earlier and Jorja spotted it immediately as he walked toward them. Under his heavy, dark eyebrows, his eyes took hers prisoner and lingered on her face. She tried to think of something to say but words escaped her. This was it. Their time was now.

Sensing what was to come, her eyes filled with tears and she looked sideways at Ben.

Each refusing to give Sokolov the satisfaction of seeing the pain in their eyes, Ben and Jorja held their gaze, resolute to face death's dark welcome together. In the hollow, cold underground space they heard Sokolov's finger pull back the hammer of his revolver, waited for the firing pin to slam against the cylinder that would discharge the first bullet, each expecting them to be first.

Gustav yelled, "No, please, stop!" But the thunderous clapping of the gunshot echoed through the space and instantly silenced Gustav's pleas.

Jorja's body shook uncontrollably when she realized Sokolov had shot and killed Gustav. Tears tightened her throat as she fought back the urge to explode into a sobbing mess. She will not give Sokolov the vengeful satisfaction he had been seeking, even if she choked to death on her fear.

Resolved in the knowledge that Ben would most probably be next, she shut her eyes and prayed that God forgave her for her part in it all, and that He would meet them both on the other side.

Want to read more? <u>One-click Shadow of Fear now!</u>

GET YOUR FREE CHRISTIAN MYSTERY!

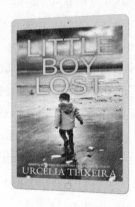

A MISSING BOY. A TOWN BURIED IN SECRETS. A DEPUTY WHO WON'T QUIT.

books.urcelia.com/little-boy-lost

MORE BOOKS BY URCELIA TEIXEIRA

PICK A BUNDLE FOR MASSIVE SAVINGS exclusive to my online store!
Save up to 50% off plus get an additional 10% discount coupon.
Visit https://shop.urcelia.com

More books coming soon! Sign up to my newsletter to be notified of new releases, giveaways and pre-release specials.

MESSAGE FROM THE AUTHOR

All glory be to the Lord, my God who breathed every word through me onto these pages.

I have put my words in your mouth and
covered you with the shadow of My hand
Isaiah 51:16

It is my sincere prayer that you not only enjoyed the story, but drew courage, inspiration, and hope from it, just as I did while writing it. Thank you sincerely, for reading *Vengeance is Mine*.

I appreciate your help in spreading the word, including telling a friend. Reviews help readers find books! Please leave a review on your favorite book site.

Writing without distractions is a never-ending challenge. With a house full of boys, there's never a dull moment (or a quiet one!)

So I close myself off and shut the world out by popping in my earphones.

Here's what I listened to while I wrote *Vengeance is Mine*:

- 10 Hours/God's Heart Instrumental Worship—Soaking in His presence (https://youtu.be/Yltj6VKX7kU)
- 2 Hours Non-Stop Worship Songs—Daughter of Zion (https://youtu.be/DKwcFiNe7xw)

When I finished writing the last sentence of the book!
How great is our God—Chris Tomlin
(https://youtu.be/KBD18rsVJHk)

ABOUT THE AUTHOR

Award winning author of faith-filled Christian Suspense Thrillers that won't let you go!™

Urcelia Teixeira, writes gripping Christian mystery, thriller and suspense novels that will keep you on the edge of your seat! Firm in her Christian faith, all her books are free from profanity and unnecessary sexually suggestive scenes.

She made her writing debut in December 2017, kicking off her newly discovered author journey with her fast-paced archaeological adventure thriller novels that readers have described as 'Indiana Jones meets Lara Croft with a twist of Bourne.'

But, five novels in, and nearly eighteen months later, she had a spiritual re-awakening, and she wrote the sixth and final book in her Alex Hunt Adventure Thriller series. She now fondly refers to *The Caiaphas Code* as her redemption book. Her statement of faith. And although this series has reached multiple Amazon Bestseller lists, she took the bold step of following her true calling and switched to writing what honors her Creator: Christian Mystery and Suspense fiction.

The first book in her newly discovered genre went on to win the 2021 Illumination Awards Silver medal in the Christian Fiction category and the series reached multiple Amazon Bestseller lists!

While this success is a great honor and blessing, all glory goes to God alone who breathed every word through her!

A committed Christian for over twenty years, she now lives by the following mantra:

"I used to be a writer. Now I am a writer with a purpose!"

For more on Urcelia and her books, visit www.urcelia.com

To walk alongside her as she deepens her writing journey and walks with God, sign up to her Newsletter - https://newsletter.urcelia.com/signup

or

Follow her on

Facebook: https://www.facebook.com/urceliabooks

Twitter: https://twitter.com/UrceliaTeixeira

BookBub: https://www.bookbub.com/authors/urcelia-teixeira

facebook.com/urceliateixeira

twitter.com/urcelia_teixeira

instagram.com/urceliateixeira

Made in the USA
Las Vegas, NV
28 February 2024

86419086R10163